ELIJAH
VISIBLE

*To Barbara & Ron,
with affection and
friendship for the*

ELIJAH
VISIBLE

STORIES BY

THANE
ROSENBAUM

noble & wife Rabbi.

[signature]

ST. MARTIN'S PRESS ⚜ NEW YORK

Excerpts from *The Little Red Lighthouse and the Great Gray Bridge* by Hildegarde H. Swift and Lynn Ward, copyright 1942 by Harcourt Brace and Company and renewed 1970 by Hildegarde H. Swift and Lynn Ward, reprinted by permission of the publisher.

Photo-illustration on the frontispiece by Hugh Shurley.

Book design by Gretchen Achilles

Library of Congress Cataloging-in-Publication Data

Rosenbaum, Thane.
    Elijah visible: stories / by Thane Rosenbaum.—1st ed.
      p. cm.
    ISBN 0-312-14325-7
    1. Children of Holocaust survivors—United States—Fiction.
2. Jews—United States—Social life and customs—Fiction.
3. Holocaust survivors—United States—Fiction. 4. Jewish families—United States—Fiction. I. Title.
PS3568.O782E44   1996
813'.54—dc20   95-52876
                                                    CIP

First Edition: April 1996
10 9 8 7 6 5 4 3 2 1

IN HONOR AND MEMORY OF

NORMAN AND BETTY ROSENBAUM,

WHOSE LIVES AND NIGHTMARES INSPIRED

THE STORIES IN THIS COLLECTION

Now nothing could ever happen good and pure enough to rub out our past . . . the scars of the outrage would remain within us for ever. . . . This is the awful privilege of our generation and of my people, no one better than us has ever been able to grasp the incurable nature of the offence, that spreads like a contagion. It is foolish to think that human justice can eradicate it. It is an inexhaustible fount of evil; it breaks the body and the spirit of the submerged, it stifles them and renders them abject; . . . it perpetuates itself as hatred among the survivors, and swarms around in a thousand ways, against the very will of all, as a thirst for revenge, as a moral capitulation, as denial, as weariness, as renunciation.

—PRIMO LEVI, *The Reawakening*

CONTENTS

ACKNOWLEDGMENTS

Bob Weil, editor, mentor, and friend, for his devotion to these stories, and for honoring me, and my work, with his vision and skill;

Becky Koh, for her gentle hands and kindness throughout the editing process;

Ellen Levine, my agent, for her guidance and conviction;

The Sarnoff family, for their ongoing encouragement and support;

Brian and Kevin O'Donoghue, and Simon Raykher, for providing me with the voices of other tribes;

Aviva Werthheimer, who thinks deeply and reads out loud;

Bruno Bier, for providing late inning heroics;

Tom Hameline, who listened for years and helped keep me sane;

Sam Rosenbaum, Shimon Vered, Esther Rosenbaum, and Pearl Rosenbaum Pantone—cousins in tragedy, and loss;

Basia Tess, who opens a new frontier of possibilities; and

Susan, who shares all the moments that really matter.

ELIJAH
VISIBLE

CATTLE
CAR
COMPLEX

He pushed the button marked "Down." He pushed again. The machine ignored the command. Slowly he pivoted his head back, staring up at the stainless-steel eyebrow just over the door. No movement of descending light. The numbers remained frozen, like a row of stalled traffic.

For bodily emphasis, he leaned against the panel—pressing "Down," "Up," "Lobby," "Open," "Close"—trying vainly to breathe some life into the motionless elevator. But there was no pulse. The car remained inert, suspended in the hollow lung of the skyscraper.

"Help!" he yelled. "Get me out of here!" The echo of his own voice returned to him.

Still no transit. The elevator was stuck on 17. A malfunctioning car with a mind for blackjack.

"Remain calm," he reminded himself. "I'll push the emergency alarm."

Then he saw a conspicuous red knob that jutted out more prominently than all the other buttons. Adam reached and pulled. A pulsating ring shook the car and traveled down the shaft, triggering a flood of memories he had buried inside him. He covered his ears; a briefcase dropped to the floor.

"That should reach them," he said, running his hand through his hair, trying to relax.

It was late, well past midnight. Adam Posner had been working on a motion for court the next day. Out his window the lights of the Manhattan skyline glittered with a radiance that belied the stillness of the hour.

A lawyer's life, connected to a punchless carousel of a clock.

He hated being among them—being *one* of them—with their up-scale suits and shallow predicaments; those conveniently gymnas-tic ethical values, bending and mutating with the slightest change of financial weather. Gliding by colleagues in the corridors, walk-ing zombies with glazed eyes and mumbling mouths. No time to exchange pleasantries. That deathly anxiety over deadlines—the ex-haust of a tireless treadmill, legs moving fleetingly, furiously.

He played the game reluctantly, knowing what it was doing to his spirit, but also painfully aware of his own legacy, and its con-tribution to the choices he was destined to make. Above all else he wanted to feel safe, and whatever club offered him the privilege of membership, he was duty-bound to join.

And so another night on the late shift. He was working on be-half of a lucrative client, his ticket to a partnership at the firm. He was the last attorney or staff member to leave that night, something he always sought to avoid. Adam didn't like being alone in dark places, and he didn't like elevators—especially when riding alone.

Some of the lights in the interior hallway had been turned off, leaving a trail of soft shadows along the beige, spotless carpet. His Hermés tie, with the new fleur-de-lis pattern, was hanging from his neck in the shape of a noose, and the two top buttons of his shirt stayed clear of their respective eyelets. A warrior of late-night occupations.

There was a car waiting for him downstairs, one of those plush Lincolns that cater to New York's high-salaried slaves. When he entered the elevator, he could think of nothing but returning to his apartment building, commandeering yet another elevator, and ris-ing to his honeycombed domain overlooking the Empire State Building. He lived alone in a voiceless, sanitized shrine—his very own space in the sky. Not even a pet greeted him, just the hum of an empty refrigerator filled with nothing but a half-empty carton of ice cream, a solitary microwave dinner, and a box of baking soda.

Sleep. How desperately he wanted to sleep. But now the night would take longer to end, and sleep was not yet possible.

"Behave rationally," he said, a lawyerly response to a strained situation. "They'll come and get me. At the very least, they'll need to get the elevator back," he reasoned.

Then with a nervous thumb, he stabbed away at the panel in all manner of chaotic selection. At that moment, any floor, any longitude, would do. Defeated by the inertia of the cab, he ran his hands against the board as though he were playing a harp, palms floating over waves of oval buttons and coded braille, searching for some hidden escape hatch.

The dimensions of the car began to close in on him. The already tight space seemed to be growing smaller, a shrinking enclosure, miniaturizing with each breath.

Adam's parents had been in the camps, transported there by rail, cattle cars, in fact. That was a long time ago, another country, another time, another people. An old, trite subject—unfit for dinnertime discussion, not in front of the children, not the way to win friends among Gentiles. The Holocaust fades like a painting exposed to too much sun. A gradual diminishing of interest—once the rallying cry of the modern Diaspora; now like a freak accident of history, locked away in the attic, a hideous Anne Frank, trotted out only occasionally, as metaphorical mirror, reminding those of what was once done under the black eye of indifference.

Adam himself knew a little something about tight, confining spaces. It was unavoidable. The legacy that flowed through his veins. Parental reminiscences had become the genetic material that was to be passed on by survivors to their children. Some family histories are forever silent, transmitting no echoes of discord into the future. Others are like seashells, those curved volutes of the mind—the steady drone of memory always present. All one needs to do is press an ear to the right place. Adam had often heard the screams of his parents at night. Their own terrible visions from a haunted past became his. He had inherited their perceptions of space, and the knowledge of how much one needs to live, to hide, how to breathe where there is no air.

He carried on their ancient sufferings without protest—

feeding on the milk of terror; forever acknowledging—with himself as living proof—the umbilical connection between the unmurdered and the long buried.

All his life he had suffered from bouts of claustrophobia, and also a profound fear of the dark. He refused to find his way into a movie theater when a film was already in progress; not even a sympathetic usher could rid him of this paralyzing impasse. At crowded parties he always kept to the door, stationed at the exit, where there was air, where he knew he could get out.

Condemned to living a sleepless nightmare, he began to pace like an animal. His breath grew stronger and more jagged. He tore his glasses from his face and threw them down on the elevator floor. An unbalanced goose step shattered the frames, scattering the pieces around him. Dangling in the air and trapped in a box, a braided copper cable held him hostage to all his arresting fears.

"Where are they? Isn't there someone at the security desk?" He undid yet another shirt button, slamming a fist against the wall. The car rattled with the sound of a screaming saw. He yanked against the strip of a guardrail. It refused to budge. With clenched fists he punched as many numbers of random floors as his stamina allowed, trying to get through to the other side without opening a door. Ramming his head against the panel, he merely encountered the steely panel of unsympathetic buttons. The tantrum finally ended with the thrust of an angry leg.

Adam's chest tightened. A surge of anxiety possessed him. His mind alternated between control and chaos, trying to mediate the sudden emptiness. His eyes lost focus, as though forced to experience a new way of seeing. He wanted to die, but would that be enough? What had once been a reliably sharp and precise lawyer's mind rapidly became undone, replaced by something from another world, from another time, the imprinting of his legacy. Time lost all sensation; each second now palpable and deafening.

"Hel . . . p! Help!"

The sweat poured down his face in sheaths of salt, and the deepening furrows in his forehead assumed a most peculiar epidermal geometry. In abject surrender, with his back against the wall of the car, he slid down to his ankles and covered his face with his hands. Nerves had overtaken his sanity. He was now totally at the mercy of those demons that would deprive him of any rational thought. And he had no one but himself to blame; the psychic pranks of his deepest monstrous self had been summoned, reducing him to a prisoner within the locked walls of the elevator.

Suddenly a voice could be heard, glib scratches filtering through a metallic strainer built right into the panel.

"Hello, hello, are you all right in der, son?"

The voice of God? Adam wondered. So silent at Auschwitz, but here, shockingly, in the elevator—delivered with a surprisingly lilting pitch. An incomprehensible choosing of divine intervention.

"It's the night guard from the lobby. Can ya hear me?"

Adam looked up to the ceiling. He squinted, trying to make out the shapes and sounds of rescue amidst an evolving fog of subconscious turmoil.

"Can ya hear me?" an urgent male voice persisted in reaching him. The voice carried the melody of an Irishman from an outer borough, but Adam, unaccountably, heard only a strident German.

"Yes, I am here," Adam replied, absently, weakly, almost inaudibly.

"Are ya all right?"

"No."

"We 'ave a situation 'ere," the security guard said calmly. "The motor to the elevator is jam'd. I can't repair it from 'ere; so I've called the maint'nance people. There's a fire in another buildin' downtown; and they're busy wit' dat. They said they'll be here as soon as humanly possible. Will you be okay, son?"

Adam lifted himself to his feet, pressed his mouth against the intercom—a static current startled his face—and then screamed: "What do you mean by 'okay'? How can I be okay? This is not life—

being trapped in a box made for animals! Is there no dignity for man?" After another pause, he wailed, "You are barbarians! Get me out!"

The guard's lips pursed with all due bewilderment, and his tone sank. "You 'aven't been inside der long, mister. I know ya want to get out and go home for de night, but let's not make this a bigger ordeal than it already 'tis."

Adam then volunteered the nature of this "ordeal."

"Why should we be forced to resettle? This is our home. We are Germans! We have done nothing wrong! Nazis! Murderers! Nazis!"

The lobby of the building was barren, the only sound the quiet gurgle of water dripping down the side of a Henry Moore fountain. The stark marble walls were spare. The interior lights dimmed for the evening.

The security guard pondered Adam's reply, and then muttered to himself: "It takes all kinds. The elevator gets stuck, and he calls *me* a Nazi. Who told him to labor so long? Goddamn yuppie, asshole." Recovering, he picked up the receiver and said, "I'm sorry, sir. I don't get your meanin'. Say, ya got a German in der wit' ya?"

"We can't breathe in here! And the children, what will they eat? How can we dispose of our waste? We are not animals! We are not cattle! There are no windows in here, and the air is too thin for all of us to share. You have already taken our homes. What more do you want? Please give us some air to breathe."

By now the guard was joined by the driver of the limousine, who had been parked on Third Avenue waiting for Adam to arrive. The driver, a Russian émigré, had grown anxious and bored, staring out onto an endless stream of yellow cabs; honking fireflies passing into the night, heading uptown. By radio he called his dispatcher, trying to find out what had happened to his passenger, this Mr. Posner, this lawyer who needed the comforts of a plush sedan to travel thirty blocks back to his co-op. The dispatcher knew of no cancellation. Adam Posner was still expected downstairs to claim his ride. This was America after all, the driver mused. The elite take their time and leave others waiting.

So the driver left his car to stretch his legs. Electronically activated doors opened as he entered the building and shuffled over a burnished floor to a circular reception pedestal. The security guard was still struggling to communicate with Adam.

"I am looking for a Mr. Posner," the driver said, with Russian conviction. "I should pick him up outside, and to drive him to Twenty-ninth Street, East Side. Do you know this man?"

With a phone cradled under his chin, and a disturbed expression on his face, the guard said, "All I know is we have an elevator down, and at least one man stuck inside. But who knows who—or what—else he's got in der with 'im. I tink he's actin' out parts in a play. To tell you the truth, he sounds a bit daft to me."

With the aplomb of a police hostage negotiator, the Russian said, "Let me talk to him. I'll find out who he is." The guard shrugged as the phone changed hands. The Russian removed his angular chauffeur's cap and wiped his brow. A determined expression seized his face as he lifted the cradle to his mouth, and said, "Excuse me. Is a Mr. Posner in there?"

"What will become of the women and children?" Adam replied. "Why should we be resettled in Poland?" He did not wait for a reply. A brief interlude of silence was then followed by a chorus of moans and shrieks, as if a ward in a veterans' hospital had become an orchestra of human misery, tuning up for a concert. "I don't believe they are work camps! We won't be happy. We will die there! I can feel it!"

The Russian was himself a Jew and winced with all too much recognition. "Is this Mr. Posner?" he continued. "This is your limo. Don't worry, we will get you out. We will rescue you."

Adam now heard this man from Brighton Beach with his Russian accent, the intoned voice of liberation. Who better to free him from his bondage than a Bolshevik from the east—in this case from Minsk or Lvov—the army that could still defeat the Germans.

"Liberate us! We are starving! We are skeletons, walking bones, ghosts! Get us out of this hell!"

"What's 'e sayin'?" the security guard asked.

"I'm not exactly sure, but I think it has something to do with the Holocaust, my friend."

"Ah, de Holycost; a terrible thing, dat."

The Russian nodded—the recognition of evil, a common language between them. "I'll talk to him again," he said, and grabbed the intercom again. "Mr. Posner, don't worry. We will get you out. You are not in camps. You are not in cattle car. You are just inside elevator, in your office building. You are a lawyer; you've worked late. You are tired, and scared. You must calm down."

"Calm down, calm down, so easy for you Russians to say," Adam replied, abruptly. "We have been selected for extermination. We cannot survive. Who will believe what has happened to us? Who will be able to comprehend? Who will say kaddish for me?"

The lobby was crowding up. Two drowsy-looking repairmen, their sleep disturbed by the downtown fire and now this, entered the building and went up to the guard console. "What's the problem here?" one of them asked. "We're with the elevator company."

Fully exasperated, the guard indignantly replied, "Ya want to know what's wrong, do ya? Ya want to know what the *problem* is? I'll tell ya! It's supposed to be de graveyard shift. Piece o' cake, they say, nothin' ever happens, right? Not when I'm on duty. No, sir. When I'm 'ere, graveyard means all the ghosts come out, the mummies, the wackos! We 'ave a loony tune stuck in one o' the elevators!" Jauntily, winking at one of the maintenance men, he added, "I think de guy in de elevator thinks he's in some fuckin' World War Two movie."

"This man in elevator is not crazy," the Russian driver said in defense. "It is world that is crazy; he is only one of its victims. Who knows what made him like this?"

One of the repairmen dashed off to the control room. Moments later he returned, carrying a large mechanical device, an extraction that would bring the night to an end and allow everyone to go home. "I think I fixed the problem," he announced. "It was just a jammed crank."

As he was about to finish explaining the exploits behind the repair, the elevator began its appointment with gravity. The four men moved from the center of the lobby and gathered in front of the arriving elevator car.

"Should we ring an ambulance?" the security guard wondered. "I hope I don't lose me wages over this. I've done all anyone could. You know," he gestured toward the limousine driver, "you were here." The driver refused to take his eyes off the blinking lights, the overhead constellation that signaled the car's gradual descent.

The elevator glided to a safe stop. Like a performer on opening night, the car indulged in a brief hesitation—a momentary hiccup, of sorts—before the doors opened.

As the elevator doors separated like a curtain, the four men, in one tiny choreographed step, edged closer to the threshold, eager to glimpse the man inside. Suddenly there was a collective shudder, and then a retreat.

The unveiling of Adam Posner.

Light filtered into the car. The stench of amassed filth was evident. It had been a long journey. An unfathomable end.

Adam was sitting on the floor, dressed in soiled rags. Silvery flecks of stubble dappled his bearded face. Haltingly, he stared at those who greeted him. Were they liberators or tormentors? He did not yet know. His eyes slowly adjusted to the light, as though his confinement offered nothing but darkness. He presented the men of the transport with an empty stare, a vacancy of inner peace. As he lifted himself to his feet, he reached for a suitcase stuffed with a life's worth of possessions, held together by leather straps fastened like rope. Grabbing his hat and pressing it on his head, Adam emerged, each step the punctuation of an uncertain sentence. His eyes were wide open as he awaited the pronouncement: right or left, in which line was he required to stand?

ROMANCING
THE
YOHRZEIT
LIGHT

The sizzle from an ignited match always revived the same memory.

With her face bathed softly in light, Esther would rotate the fire with two steady, benevolent hands, blessing the end of yet another week, and the beginning of Shabbat.

She was a short woman, with dark hair and light skin. He remembered how her small frame appeared to be a liability before each Friday night benediction. But she was resourceful, a survivor of the Holocaust; a tall table and long candles were no match for her. She would prop herself on her toes for the actual kindling, then drop down again.

Pressing her palms gently over her closed eyelids, she would then entrust the soul with the task of sight. A beige, embroidered veil, which had concealed her features, by now was raised and folded over her hair. She would stare off into some dark, spiritual galaxy. Her lips trembled, and from her mouth came a melody of ancient Hebrew hymns, delivered in a faint, garbled whisper, so that even God would have trouble hearing.

Then, with eyes still closed, she would cast out her arms in some confused abandon, the performance of some modified breaststroke that brought the flames closer together. The lights from the candles would dance joyously on her face, shining upon her in some angelic way, transcending the mere commencement of the Sabbath.

All this, and the haunting vision of the memory it produced, caused a deep lament in Adam on the first anniversary of his mother's death. The mettle of a loving son was about to be measured by the flick of his own wrist, as the faithful alchemy of fire and wax passed on to the next generation.

By Jewish law, each year, on the same day that she died, he was required to light one candle in her memory. The *yohrzeit,* Jews call it. It was to be no ordinary candle, either, but rather one capable of burning for twenty-four hours without interruption.

Despite his deep affection for his mother, Adam was bereft of her spiritual wisdom; he had inherited none of Esther's ability to commune with Friday's flames. On the day marking Esther's first *yohrzeit,* it became sadly apparent how the obligations and rituals of his faith competed—all too unsuccessfully—against the blasphemy to which he had grown accustomed.

Adam's relationship with his mother had never been easy when she was alive; now, after her death, her candle wasn't about to cooperate, either.

At first he wasn't sure about the correct date on which this all was to take place. According to the Christian calendar, Esther had died on October 16, but for Jews there was some altogether different configuration of sun and moon that fashioned the days and months of the year. The Hebrew date was bound to be different, perhaps by a week or maybe more—in any direction, no less. Adam was at a complete loss as to how to arrive at some symmetry between these competing calendars. In the absence of user-friendly conversion charts, he simply resigned himself to performing his rite of Jewish remembrance according to the only days of the year that he knew.

As midnight approached on October 16, Adam frantically realized that he did not own a *yohrzeit* candle.

"Just great," he muttered, flipping through a kitchen drawer filled with wires, playing cards, and assorted rubber bands. "I've got these birthday candles, but they won't last for a whole day, even if I stand here and light them one at a time," he thought.

He eyed a cupboard that had been relegated to storing the odds and ends that never got used in his life, or art. Standing on the counter like a child searching for an advance on the evening's cookie allowance, he found a long, opaque cylinder filled with equal layers of kaleidoscopic wax—the kind of mood maker that might service a temporary power outage quite well.

"This might last for a whole day," he said quizzically, "but I need something that rabbis would approve of—something with a kosher U on it, or a circle with a pig's face exxed out right on the front. What else is in here?" He fumbled nervously with all sorts of unmeltable objects, slamming cabinets and clanging anything that happened to get in his way.

But the candles were the least of his problems. He lived among so many unkosher influences both in and out of his apartment, that the lighting of the *yohrzeit* candle—albeit a solid gesture and a good beginning—would not have redressed the multitude of sins he committed daily. He could no longer be redeemed. After a lifetime of going too far it wasn't even clear whether his god, or his people, even wanted him back.

Esther had raised him in an Americanized kosher home—observance within the threshold, nutritional anarchy outside. But he had slackened the already compromised routine well beyond the acceptable limits. He ate all manner of spineless fish, and the commingled flesh of unhoofed animals. His hot dogs didn't answer to a higher authority other than his own whim of which sidewalk peddler to patronize.

His neighborhood on the Upper West Side was filled with synagogues, but Adam acted as though they were virtual leper colonies—cursed concrete structures set in between the familiar brownstones, to be avoided at all cost. He never celebrated Rosh Hashanah (actually, he couldn't tell you exactly what time of the year it even was). During the fall, when fashionably dressed Jewish families all over Manhattan rushed to services, Adam blankly assumed the coincidence of various nearby, midweek weddings. Instead, he welcomed the New Year on January 1, in Central Park at the stroke of twelve, jogging soberly in the Midnight Run, his body aglow under mushroom clouds of bursting fireworks.

Recently he had fallen in love with yet another in an unending series of Gentile women. All were very beautiful, taller than Adam, and from parts of the world that he had never visited. The conversations were brief, the relationships even shorter. Misbegotten romances guided by primal, rather than tribal, considerations.

If Adam's taste in women wanted to conform to the preferences of his people—or the hopes of his mother—a nice Jewish girl could easily have been found; but it wasn't as though Jewish girls were much interested in him, either. They looked upon him as though he were a *sheygets,* often surprised to learn that he was Jewish at all.

Adam had the rugged look of a Nordic caveman. To locate the physical attributes of *his* species, he would have had more luck at the Museum of Natural History than any other place on the West Side. For one thing, his arms were well out of proportion with the rest of his body. They were long, and seemed to hang down to the ground from his five-eight frame. He had long blond hair that was thick and uncombed, and a grayish beard that couldn't decide what purpose to play on his face. His eyes were large and blue, overwhelming a pair of round, small-framed glasses that looked as though he had just picked them off the street. His nose was small and impractical. Generally speaking, a far cry from the more typical Hebrew violinist or plastic surgeon.

What's more, professionally, he was a painter—an abstract expressionist, no less. Although he was a successful downtown artist, represented by one of the more tony Soho galleries, that was not quite enough for the Daughters of Jerusalem. Naturally, they would want a more stable lifestyle, seeking the comforts of a West End Avenue co-op, a summer house on the Island, and a standing smoked fish order from Zabar's.

Gentile women from foreign countries, on the other hand, appreciated something in Adam that the women of his own tribe had missed. Adam had that threatening, reckless quality that draws people to New York in the first place. He lived in on the top floor of a five-floor walk-up, with no doorman. He rode a motorcycle. His fingernails were polished with either black greasepaint or some other dark acrylic. His hands perpetually smelled as though they had just been lathered in turpentine.

Adam offered himself to these women as their first great American fling; a nice way to be introduced to the mania of New York. After that, they would be gone, and he would be in search of still another romantic traveler.

Now there was Tasha Haglund, newly arrived from Malmö and working in New York as a fashion model for the Ford Agency. The first time he met her Adam felt that something was different—not just in her, but in him as well. The setting itself was a change of pace. It wasn't at one of those phantom Manhattan parties, arranged by the roving downtown elite. Adam knew them well, the kind of inbred gathering that would be suffocating to anyone except those with the airy ambitions of the casually hip. Tasha he met at Barnes & Noble, uptown. She was reading Günter Grass; he was staring at compositions in a book that contained the paintings of Anselm Kiefer.

"I very much like Kiefer," she said, as a way of introduction. Adam had been sitting on the floor; Tasha kneeled down beside him. "I saw one of his shows in Berlin. His paintings are so filled with modern despair. What do you think?"

He couldn't think. Who was she? Where does such a person come from? She was a typical-looking Swede: the blond hair, the blue eyes, the robust smile, the velvety skin tone. Modeling agencies scout these women zealously, then import them to America like ski equipment.

But here again Tasha was different. In a curious way, she looked a little like Adam; their hair and skin color almost matched, although Adam was always in a need of a shampoo and a shave. She even had long arms, just like his.

"I miss home. I feel lost in New York."

"So do I."

"But isn't this where you are from?"

*   *   *

Hopelessly aware of Adam's fidelity to a certain species of flesh, Esther never hesitated to offer her own wishes for his romantic future. "You need to find someone who knows who you are and understands where you come from."

"I think it's a little late for that, don't you think?" he would say, not very reassuringly. "I'm not even sure who I am, or where I come from."

Whenever speaking with Esther about such matters, he always tried to paint right through the experience. At that moment in the conversation, he was splashing paint around liberally, embellishing a pulverized Coke can that he had tarred right onto the canvas.

"*Ach*, ever since your father died—one rebellion after another. Running away from who you are. Pretending to be someone else. Who do you think you are fooling?"

"Pretty much everybody but you. You're a tough one."

"I didn't survive the camps so you could walk around looking and acting like a camp guard. Look at you. Nothing Jewish that I can see."

"We've talked about this enough. I can't change. I can't be who you want. You want to live through me. You'll need to find someone else."

"Thank God your father has been dead all these years—because *this,*" she said, raising an open palm up and down, "would have killed him." She then sighed, and watched paint splatter and suffuse with other materials. Her manic son was now sweating, the veins in his wrist pulsing, the rhythm of each stroke urgent—threatening to knock the entire canvas over.

An hour before midnight. Cabs roamed the near-empty avenues, searching for fares. A few homeless men were bickering on the corner. Spanish music pounded against a closed window, muffled but still able to be heard from the street.

Adam feared that his break from his people and his infidelity to Esther's memory were about to be tested once more. But where could he find an official *yohrzeit* candle at this late hour? Regrettably, even in New York, there are no all-night Judaica convenience shops for the modern Jew on the run.

Hurriedly, he grabbed his coat and left the apartment in search of a *yohrzeit* candle. It was a chilly, luminous Manhattan night. Checkerboard windows, hanging from a brick-infested sky, signed on and off, revealing the habits of those who slept within. A cascade of unseasonable snowflakes gradually made their way down to the side streets. Adam lifted his collar and turned the corner, heading toward the Korean market on Broadway and Eighty-fifth Street. Perhaps a convenience store that housed all that emergency juice, milk, and eggs might also carry the essentials for the neglectful Jew.

As he approached the man working the counter—a short, hunched-over fellow with a round face—Adam wondered whether there was a Korean word for *yohrzeit,* something that would make his improbable request somewhat easier to reject. He inched closer to the man, as though he was going to drop the word right into his ear, not wanting anything to get lost in transmission.

"Do you have any *yohrzeit* candles?"

The man, standing behind a display of Snickers bars, blondies, and sugarless chewing gum, was guarding a computerized cash register. An elderly woman was in the back, sorting through a display of cat food. A reward for her pet, the one other breathing entity in her apartment that separated her from virtual isolation.

Much to Adam's surprise, the Korean on the late shift nodded effusively, as if some common language had been discovered. He walked out from behind the counter, grabbed hold of Adam's arm and escorted him past the tofu and the yucca, over to a shelf brimming with crackers and low-fat oatmeal cookies. At the very bottom of the shelf, seemingly tiny and humbled, and arranged neatly so as not to offend, stood a few wax-filled glasses—a wick in each, secured to the bottom by a metal clasp. A cheap gummy label was stamped decorously right on the front of each one, bearing the reverential Hebrew word YOHRZEIT.

"Wow, you have a lot of them, I see," Adam exclaimed.

The Korean, this time less enthusiastically, nodded once more.

"A lot of dead Jews around here, I guess, or just their relatives."

The Korean agreed, just as a large cat emerged from the end of the aisle.

Adam paid for the candle and left, thinking that he should have bought more—for next year, and the year after that, perhaps. But this was his first voyage of remembrance. No need to stockpile, at least not just yet. The experience might prove too painful. He could end up feeling foolish, or worse, more empty than usual. It was just a candle, after all. Wasn't there some other way to honor the dead, something that might—at the same time—help him find his way own way back, too?

With only minutes to spare before midnight, he stood in front of the dinner table, which was flush against the window, facing the back of a ten-story apartment building. Late-night neighbors, taking a break from *Letterman,* could see Adam slicing away at the side panel of a matchbox, with no result. With each thrust of his hand, his frustration grew.

"Come on, come on," he implored, as though trying to reason with this souvenir from Indochine.

One wooden match after another struck the flinted side panel, and then split in two. Finally, one match crackled and sustained a blaze, then suffocated in his hand. The next attempt took hold and remained steady, but the wick to the *yohrzeit* candle, although surrounded by the flame, refused the offering. The *yohrzeit* would not light.

"Ouch!" The flame consumed the match and reached Adam's fingers.

"Am I going to need a torch for this thing?"

But then, on the very next try, all the elements for mourning cooperated—the match lit, the *yohrzeit* relented.

"Thank God." He sighed, exhausted and now nervously giddy.

With the flame now in front of him, he stared at its inaugural motions. "What now?" he thought. "Do I just stand around for twenty-four hours?"

Adam didn't know the prayers; the kaddish remained a mystery, like a foreign language. The Hebrew vowels and consonants just wouldn't come. He may have once known them, but no longer. Lost somewhere in some cavern of memory.

The candle, though bright, did not shine on Adam in the way he had remembered similar flames gravitating toward Esther. He checked his reflection in the window for some comforting radiance; all that he saw was a sketch of his own facial shadow, giving forth a quizzical, somber look. There was an uneasy silence in the room. He continued to search his memory for some Hebrew, any Hebrew—even a nice happy Hanukkah song would do in that moment of sanctified, stupefied remembrance.

The room was dark except for the candle, which cast a playful shadow against the wall. The flame seemed to dance. A *yohrzeit* with a sense of humor.

After Esther's death, Adam had lapsed into an ungovernable depression. The world around him seemed more dark and lifeless than usual. His art began to reflect these feelings, becoming even more spasmodic; the angry expressionistic images choking the canvas, and each other. The canvases themselves took on more monstrous apocalyptic shapes and physical dimensions. Some he couldn't even get out of his studio the usual way—through the elevator or main door. They had to be lowered from the window of his downtown loft. And the representational images, well . . . they depicted burnings, famines, sicknesses, nightmares—devastations of one sort or another. The urban litter that he normally assimilated into his paintings took on a more raw and violent form—a selection that better reflected the madness of New York. Crack vials, used condoms, a doll missing its arms, a discarded pair of underwear.

Sheinman, his gallery dealer, always said about Adam's work,

"What is it with you and garbage? What do you have against throwing things out? Don't get me wrong, I love the commissions, but why not try using just paint next time?"

Esther used to put it another way: "Why not paint something Jewish, Adam? If you're not going to be a doctor or a lawyer, at least let me have a Chagall for a son."

"I can't paint a cow upside down, Mom," Adam would reply. "It's just not what I do. I know nothing about the shtetls. Never been to that part of the world. Don't really care to go."

"So paint me a nice Posner window, then," she would say, with a sigh, realizing that reaching her son—either the artist or the spiritual anarchist—was well beyond her grasp.

And it wasn't just his art that had incorporated his mood. Adam had resigned himself to a silent type of mourning. He lost weight. He couldn't sleep. The nighttime calculation of barn animals didn't seem to help, either. He stared at the ceiling, admiring the abstract contours of chipped paint, searching for some comfort beyond a roof over his head. He found himself lost, no matter where he turned.

The depression continued until the day, less than a month before, when Tasha appeared suddenly—urgently almost—at Barnes & Noble.

"Are you always this sad?" she asked at the bookstore.

He stood up, giving him—for the moment, at least—a height advantage that would be lost once she did the same. "It's been a bad year. My mother died only a few months ago."

"I'm sorry to hear that," she said, "how sad. I think I now understand. . . ." But she also seemed somewhat surprised by what may have been a uniquely American custom of sharing bereavement with even the most remote of strangers.

From that maudlin beginning, a relationship grew—but not completely to Adam's satisfaction. There was a missing sexual component to their love, which Adam, as hard as he tried, could not seem to ignore. Tasha was ruled entirely by the Swedish way of subdued emotions, even among intimates. All those inviting looks, yet faultlessly decorous and self-consciously prim. And there was the understandable cynicism too. She hadn't gotten this far unmindful of how her face seduced men and intimidated women. New in the country and suspicious of its various solicitations, Tasha refused to sleep with any man until firmly convinced that she would not awake as a spoil of carnal conquest.

"Are you a virgin?" he wanted to know after a few dates ended with nothing more intimate than his face pressed up against Tasha's closed front door.

"Of course not."

"Well then, how long am I going to have to wait? We've been seeing each other for weeks now."

"When the mood hits me, you'll be the first to know," she assured him, stroking his face gently.

Accustomed as Adam was to dating Gentiles of unsurpassable beauty—some who thought little of giving over their bodies to his craven desires—he was surprised by Tasha's resolve, and his own stamina.

But desperation often reveals itself in dramatic ways. While Adam's sex life remained on hold, waiting for Tasha's trust and desire to materialize, his art did not. He had transformed his mourning over his mother, and his yet unconsummated love for Tasha, into a reservoir of artistic output, which surprisingly began to take on a new aesthetic. He started to work in warm, bright colors, turning away from the various shades of gloomy charcoal that defined his usual work. He painted a few portraits: one of Esther, sitting in one of her favorite chairs, matronly and refined; there was another of Tasha, alone in a lush green field, the sky behind her a hazy blue; and one of himself, straddling a motorcycle, the George Washington Bridge off in the horizon.

He painted feverishly, all through the nights, and then—without almost any sleep—he continued unrelievedly, the next day.

"We've got enough here for three shows," Sheinman said. "I think you need to rest up a bit. You planning on dying?"

But the pace continued. He moved from one project to the

next. His eyes took on a burning, deep-red glow. Bathing became an afterthought. He had hardly eaten, or changed his clothes, for days. Dried blotches of paint, like lesions, were everywhere—on his face, on his shirts, on his jeans, all over his apartment and studio.

It was within this cloud of mania and deprivation that the lighting of the candle took place. Filled with a desire to mourn, and tormented by sexual frustration, Adam lit the *yohrzeit* candle. Now silenced, with nothing to say, he walked away from the vigil, hoping that further immersion in his work would deflect his thoughts from the kaddish. He once more began to paint, but soon thereafter, while wiping off a brush, a knock at the door again changed the course of the evening.

Keys jingled and fumbled at the other end. Tasha, wearing blue jeans, a white shirt, and black blazer, came in on her own.

"Sorry, I couldn't wait for you to open the door," she announced to an empty room. Burdened with suitcases and bags, she added, "I thought you might be asleep."

Tasha wasn't easily given to unannounced visits. Adam had given her a set of keys the month before, but she had yet to avail herself of this privilege, fearing that the exercise of such liberties might give rise to a misleading impression. Now, suddenly, it was precisely that impression she wanted to convey.

"Where are you?"

"Over here," Adam answered, making his way back into the living room. "What are you doing in town? Aren't you supposed to be in Miami Beach, shooting for that German catalogue I can never pronounce?"

"The shoot was over early. I decided to rush back to see you." After a pause, she observed: "Boy, you smell. What's happened?"

Normally excited to see Tasha, Adam was now disappointed by her unexpected appearance.

"Thanks for the tip. I'll shower."

"You don't seem at all excited to see me," she remarked curiously. "I came back because of you. I think it's time. The wait is over."

Adam's lustful mind sensed something different. "The wait is over," he thought. Yet this sudden stirring didn't feel quite right.

"Tonight?" he asked. "All of a sudden? What's in the drinking water down in South Beach these days?"

"I don't know. It was a gorgeous day—sunny, cool, the water as blue as a Swedish summer sky. What can I say. I got in the mood, and you have suffered enough," she said wistfully. "Let's make it a romantic evening. I stopped and bought some polenta and teriyaki chicken from the gourmet deli on my way over. I also got candles."

She looked around the room, dropping her suitcase near the couch. On the table she saw the candle, already lit. "Oh, super, you were on the same wavelength, I see. My horoscope said this would happen. Hey, wait a minute, were you expecting me, or someone else?"

"Like who?" he countered, and looked around. It was merely a *yohrzeit* light, not a candle for a seance, he thought.

"You've got a romantic candle all ready for someone," she said. "Who is it for, if not for me?"

"Romantic? You call that thing *romantic?*" But then, Adam's mind switched gears, as if the flame on the table had taken offense, and was now suddenly receding.

"Don't be silly, it's you, of course," he said, holding out his arms to Tasha, enveloping her in a hug. With her face safely camouflaged in his neck, he sneaked a peak at the *yohrzeit* not wanting to provoke any jealous rivalry between these two seemingly competitive flames.

Once secure that there was no other woman in Adam's life for whom the candle burned, Tasha cautiously moved closer to the *yohrzeit* flame. It seemed to grow hotter and stronger with her guarded advance; with each step it gained renewed strength, a fiery explosion of minute sparks, as if anticipating some strange battle that needed to be waged. With twenty-two hours still to go, the flame suddenly grew in intensity, lighting up the room with a furious incandescent swagger.

"This is such a strange candle," she noted. "Not very romantic at all, actually. I've never seen anything like this—certainly not in Sweden. It's just a block of wax in a cheap glass."

"Well, it lasts longer," Adam said unconvincingly. "When a romantic evening goes on well into the night, those dainty candles die too soon. This kind is much more economical."

"I thought Americans were wasteful."

"Not with candles. We have a special thrift about them."

"Okay, let's forget about the candle for a minute. Adam, I had a few screwdrivers on the plane," Tasha announced, "and I've missed you, I've really missed you."

He wanted to tell her that this was not the time. There were vital religious issues to consider here. She wouldn't understand at first, but he would try to explain. After all, she was an intelligent, modern European. Surely she would respect the traditions of his people—once he announced that he had a people. He would reason with her. Tomorrow would do just as well. The mood could be recaptured—he hoped. Yes, this was the day he was anticipating so anxiously. And yes, the wait had required the patience of one of Adam's biblical forebears. But even he—an all-American in Jewish irreverence—knew not to tamper with the *yohrzeit* candle. He owed something to Esther's memory; staying celibate on the anniversary of his mother's death was the least he could do.

But he wasn't crazy, either.

"Let's do it here, right here," she suggested.

"Where?"

"On the table. We'll just move the candle."

"We can't move the candle," Adam said, his eyes glancing toward the flickering *yohrzeit*. The flame seemed to bend disapprovingly, with a cool diffidence.

"Sure, why not," she said, a bit befuddled. "The table seems safe and sturdy." A hiccup, brought on by airline booze, jarred the momentary stillness. Then her head tilted back in sensual amusement.

"Because . . ." Adam stammered. But there was no completion of the thought, at least not one that was obvious. He felt anguish over Esther's botched remembrance, yet, at the same time, arousal from Tasha's advances.

"Because . . ."

"I think it will be fun. What a memory we'll have," she said. "I've never done it before on a table," she confessed, as she looked on adventurously toward the butcher block. "Have you?"

Adam faltered. "Ah . . . why no . . . at least not like this." A pause, and then, "How about we do this on another night, maybe even somewhere else?"

"What?" Tasha cried out. "You've been hanging around me for weeks. Cajoling me. Seducing me. Enticing me. Telling me how unnatural my attitude was; how much it reflected my lack of trust. So now, I race all the way back from Miami to be with you, to end our wait—and *your* suffering—and you're no longer interested! The time is now, Adam. Here, let me help you with your belt."

The Swede wanted her Jewish painter, now. On the table, no less, in front of Mom. She grabbed at Adam's fly at the same time as she threw off her blazer, dropped her jeans, and nearly ripped the T-shirt that clung stiffly to her body. While sliding on the table, she pulled Adam upon her with one hand, and she shifted the *yohrzeit* candle over a few feet with the other. Adam's eyes watched the flame gasp for life. His heart, pulsing with sexual anticipation, raced just to keep up.

Adam knew enough about the imperatives of his people to know that the *yohrzeit* flame was to remain undisturbed. As the candle shifted locations, he called out, "Esther!"

"Who's Esther?" Tasha asked.

With pants crumpled around his ankles like an accordion of denim, Adam announced nervously, "My mother."

"Do you always call out your mother's name before you make love?" she said, lying on the table, a model wearing nothing but her underwear and a curiosity about Adam's yet-unexplored sexual technique.

"Not usually," he said, panting away, concerned that such unfathomable foreplay had scared Tasha away. A confession was bound to change the already tense, awkward mood under which the lovers labored, as they danced on Esther's portable grave.

"I think that's cute," Tasha said, "thinking of your mother at a time like this. Maybe Freud was right about little boys and their mothers."

As Tasha pulled Adam upon herself again, tugging him alternately from his shoulder and shirt collar, she leaned over to her left and exhaled forcefully, her breath aimed at the *yohrzeit* candle.

"Good night, Mom," Tasha said. "You really shouldn't watch what I'm about to do to your son."

Adam closed his eyes and grimaced.

But the flame surged even more demonstrably. Tasha tried again, with the same result—the table remained illuminated by the small, stubborn candle.

"That's funny," Tasha remarked in a half pant, "the damn thing won't go out. What kind of candle is this, one of those trick ones?"

Adam realized that he wasn't going to educate this Gentile about the ways of Jewish remembrance. Not now, perhaps never. He was unequivocally caught between two worlds—sandwiched between two competing desires. A small blond table had served up two irreconcilable courses on this most emotional of evenings: a Swedish smorgasbord of temptation, juxtaposed with a paltry three ounces of scrupulous wax.

As Tasha was fast discovering, the candle appeared to be supernaturally endowed. Perhaps a Jewish mother, even one no longer of this world, is never too far away from protecting her son. Both the flame and the most excitable part of Adam's anatomy remained erect. One would have to wither.

"I'm getting tired of this," she said, craning her neck, her face growing red, her body tired from all the respiratory exertions.

"There will be nothing left of me when the fun starts." Tasha puffed away at the candle as if it were a birthday cake resistant to childhood wishes.

With frustration growing, Tasha grabbed a coffee saucer and placed it over the *yohrzeit,* suffocating it irrevocably.

Once the candle went out, Adam permitted himself to relax. What was he to do, after all? The *yohrzeit* flame had met a premature demise. Not such a big tragedy in this world. It was a false start; his period of mourning ended suddenly. Adam's need for Tasha's body had abbreviated the anniversary of his mother's death. Esther would have to wait until next year. Maybe there is no return from the dead.

Suddenly, Adam's sexual technique seemed more adroit then before. Sexual restraint went the same way of spiritual observance. A butcher-block table was transformed into a palace of divine passion. Human legs dangled beside wooden ones, Tasha and Adam's limbs kicking wildly into the air; animal noises, grunts and groans, screamed from a now shadowless room.

Three weeks later Tasha formally moved into Adam's apartment. The aborted *yohrzeit* candle had by now become an indistinct memory, but the evidence of its ruin would remain forever with him. Using a small spatula, Adam had removed the unused wax, then pulverized the glass into crystal shards, which he slapped upon a canvas that he intended to paint entirely in black. It was to be a celestial scene of bright stars amidst a universal void. He had returned to his old melancholy, but familiar, form.

Christmas was approaching, Tasha's first in America. Manhattan was cooperating for the occasion. Central Park was covered with a light layer of snow. Holiday smells muscled their way into the grimy air. Shoppers slammed into one another on the streets and in the stores with few of their customary snarls—a New Yorker's way of demonstrating peace on earth and goodwill toward fellow men.

Tasha brought home a handsome evergreen—a Douglas fir to be exact—Adam's first Christmas tree.

"We can do this, right?" she asked.

"Why not?"

"I don't know what happens to Jewish boys on their first Christmas."

"Well, we'll just find out."

Adam watched Tasha's excited face as she carefully unpacked a box of dainty decorations that she had brought over with her from Malmö. As she unwrapped them, she lifted them up one by one, and guided by some ornamental instinct, attached each of them to the tree. An angel. A gingerbread man. A Christmas ram made of straw. A reindeer. A Swedish Santa—the *juletomte,* also dressed in red. Hand-carved wooden hearts. There were a few gremlins and a grimacing troll. And an entire assortment of woven baskets, filled with homemade candies and caramels wrapped in holiday paper, which weighed down the branches with a colorful harvest.

"This is always my favorite season," she confessed, searching each limb for a desirable resting place. "Back home in Sweden, my whole family would love it when Father would hoist up that great big tree we had every year."

"Sounds nice," Adam would say, cheerily, repeating to himself *she's so gorgeous,* in rhapsodic justification.

She had prepared a traditional Swedish Christmas eve smorgasbord of smoked ham, dried white codfish, and for dessert, *julgrot,* which, he was to learn, was a porridge of cooked rice.

"You know, there is an almond in the *julgrot.* Back in Sweden, the person who gets the almond in their portion is said to be the first to get married."

"There's only two of us here. I guess we can't lose."

"This makes me feel so at home. Now, where's that angel?"

Adam smiled, the sides of his mouth turning slightly upwards. But where was *his* home, he wondered quietly?

The Swedish Christmas carol, *"Nu Ar Det Jul Igen,"* resonated throughout the apartment, played on a CD that her sister had sent in a holiday care package. The melody was upbeat, but the lyrics seemed harsh. Of course, Adam didn't understand any Swedish, yet. So he simply let the music transport him wherever it wanted. He lay beside the tree, shifting already-wrapped presents around in tidy arrangement. Tasha's face reflected a swelling of Yuletide anticipation that he had never known.

She found her angel, lodged in the bottom of the box, preserved carefully in tissue paper. This angel was silver, with a big holder on the top of one of the wings for a candle. She stepped on a chair, then arched on her toes for that extra boost, rising above the highest point of the tree, and added the final touch. The angel stood poised at the summit like a saintly crown. A match sizzled, and she lit the candle, placing it gently inside the angel. Adam watched silently as Tasha remained on the chair, crying blissfully, her face a splendid glow, resurrecting her childhood here on West Eighty-seventh Street in Manhattan. As the night wore on, Adam fell asleep beside the Christmas tree, curled up like an unwrapped present, a lifeless ornament, the keeper of the flame.

THE
PANTS
IN THE
FAMILY

The father's grip loosened, and out slipped the tiny hand. A sun-drenched boardwalk revealed a shadow of yawning fingers; jagged limbs dancing on the ashen boards. The child was left alone on the boardwalk. Fallen cargo. Unclaimed goods. Encircled by a blur of tall, driven, unending legs; the ceaseless ebb and flow of adult frenzy. Seagulls swirled overhead, surrendering to the breezy currents of the morning sky—the only witnesses to the human abandonment below.

It all started with the invitation from a stranger, a dare from a man who profited from such amusements.

"Hey, mister, want to take a chance?" the barker asked casually, motioning to the father. "Test your skill, test your luck!"

The barker was a husky man with a moon face, cratered with pockmarks and red gashes, the result of several reckless shaving episodes. A great belly hung from his belt—an absurd tumor. His black hair was matted tight with the gloss of shoe polish.

Father and son had been strolling hand in hand along the Atlantic City boardwalk, passing one arcade after another. On either side of them stood the decrepit shelters of these games of chance— beckoning with an ominous allure. There was a guesser of weight, masking his eyes with open palm; a man juggling hollow baseballs, standing beside a sculpture of steel flasks; a leopard-suited behemoth lifting a hammer the size of an anvil and repeatedly trouncing a wearied bell. Across the way, Ping-Pong balls danced on the thin necks of regimented lime-green bottles, set a strategic distance apart; a pie thrower stepped back like an angry waiter; a reader of tarot cards bent over a cheap table, shrouded in gypsy costume.

Each arcade had a gray cast that even the sun could not

brighten. Faces seemed rubbery and elastic. Rarely would any of those assorted projectiles find their targets; there was little contest to these games of chance. The odds were in the vendors' favor. The people would leave disappointed.

Wheels clicked away, spinning endlessly, keeping time to the plaintive tunes of all this artifice. Disarmed guns went off in unison. The ocean returned an echo of elated shouts and dejected moans—the folly of near-misses and almost-hads, and the occasional stuffed animal trophy.

It was that ambivalent time of year, just when the summer began its retreat and the leaves betrayed the first traces of autumn. The wind kissed the swells of the ocean, and far away, clouds were hanging low. A misty blanket of covert rain gathered underneath.

Atlantic City always had the instincts for betting. Before the glittering gambling palaces—the blinding makeover that transported a Nevada desert to the Jersey shore—there was the boardwalk. A long stretch of wood, battered by stormy winds and the almost invisible workings of corrosive salt. Just a carnival, without the casinos. No weekend junkets or courtesy cocktails; the unaddicted blue collar was, in those days, more interested in bowling than baccarat.

"People been ice-cold all day. Can't hit a thing," the barker continued with a cynical, baiting tone. His place of business was a redwood shed that faced the ocean on the opposite side of the railing that bordered the sand. Stuffed animals, each with the same vacant stare, dangled from the roof and rested along shelves. Behind him, an assembly of crass targets. "You look like a crack shot. Try your luck, test your skill. Win something for the kid."

The man held up a rifle and then tossed it in the air, catching the barrel, which he then balanced against his palm. His belly jiggled throughout the seduction.

"Come on," he motioned, "show your kid what you're made of. . . ."

Father and son walked away, angling in the direction of alternate diversions. The rumble of crashing waves threatened to drown out the barker just as he began to say, "Your kid will remember this day, when his pop chickened out of a fight. He won't forget, the yellow of his old man!"

Within moments they returned, back to the scene of the barker's unpardonable taunt, which echoed in the father's ear as though broadcast from the ocean. He took long, purposeful strides, dragging the child, whose feet scraped and clattered along the boards. The father let go of the son's hand, replacing it with the rifle. He measured carefully—knowing its body, familiar with its fury. With his left hand he caressed the barrel, running his hand over the top—gently, soothingly, calming the quiver. The father then shunted his neck to the side to relieve an anxious tick, cocked the rifle, and unleashed a stream of shells, which followed one another faithfully, each with an assigned mission.

The singular movement set off shot after shot, whistling through the air, creating an unbelievable carnage: upended saucer dishes; once rotating ceramic birds, stunned into submission; swirling red-faced bull's-eyes, all falling in the father's ambush.

"Jesus!" the barker exclaimed, wiping his forehead, smoothing out petrified furrows. "I thought you were a pigeon, never had you figured for such a dead shot. You in the army or something?"

The father laid the rifle down on the table. Wisps of tangled smoke wrestled in the air, then faded.

The trance was over. "Where's my boy?" he asked, searching the boardwalk. "Did you see him? Where did he go?"

"Forget the kid," the barker said, handing the father the largest stuffed bear in the kingdom. "Hey, where you going? Come back! How's about double or nothing?"

He was a man of great mystery, but sitting there in the waiting room of the hospital, his wife falling under the spell of etheric gas, his nerves worn thin from overuse, he looked neither mysterious, nor like someone capable of hearing bad news. So the task fell to me. The obligations of fatherhood passed on to the son before either had the chance to settle into their more conventional assignments.

.   "Is a Mr. Posner here?" a doctor wearing an aqua surgical tunic called out.

"Yes, that's me," I answered.

The doctor measured my response, then removed a mask that dropped from his neck.

"Aren't you a little young to be Mr. Posner?"

There was cause for skepticism. I was still a sophomore at the Windsor School in Connecticut, very much smooth-faced, awkward in my movements, not sure whether to fold my arms or slip my hands inside my pockets. My unhesitating claims to maturity were sorely unconvincing. The "mister" in me was there—nurtured by an accelerated childhood—but the outward appearance of adolescence betrayed all other sources of development.

"Actually," I said, "the real Mr. Posner is there," pointing toward the back of the room, where my father was sitting, unmindful of anyone else in the room, including me.

"Then who are you supposed to be?"

The doctor was tall with a thin unsmiling face. His hair was cut short, his eyes a distracted, arrogant blue. He had a cold manner about him, whether it be by bedside, or waiting room.

A clot of blood had seeped deeply into the fibers of the surgeon's uniform. This wasn't all that uncommon, I supposed, for a profession that tangled in bodily trenches. But there was a nauseating sense that this specimen was not from an anonymous donor.

"I'm the son—of the man back there, and the lady under the knife," I replied.

"I see. Well, if you'll excuse me, I should go over and discuss matters with your father."

"Wait!" I urged, grabbing hold of the doctor's smock. "Can I talk to you for a second?"

"Really, I should be moving along," he said hastily, annoyed.

"Your mother is in surgery down the hall. I just need to explain a few things to your father."

"Explain them to me," I insisted.

"It really should be your father."

"Leave him alone, he won't be able to handle it," I said, in a manner that revealed nothing of the sophomore. "The man's been through enough. He's old, and weak, and has been disappointed before by bad news. Just look at him . . . what else do you need to know?"

The doctor's knowledge of our family was incomplete. Not his fault, really. A microscope can reveal only so much, its analysis confined to cellular structure, alone. His patient had survived the camps. Her husband had the same curriculum vitae. Eventually, luck always runs out.

"What was the family's medical history?"

"No way to know," I replied. "Everyone was killed—on both sides. The bodies never got the chance to live out their natural lives. I guess you could say our genes are susceptible only to murder."

The doctor stared impassively. He had heard enough. He was fidgeting with his mask, turning his head from side to side, wanting to return to the operating room, which now, by comparison, seemed so comforting and safe.

"All right, I think I understand," he said. "Why don't you sit down?"

"I'm fine standing," I said, although the knees had their own insight about my steadiness. "Go ahead, doctor, tell me," I said, with all the maturity a sixteen-year-old could summon. I leaned against the wall as a precaution.

"Your mother's condition is a little worse than we had suspected. We had hoped to find something else—gallstones or a stricture blocking the bile duct—but I'm afraid she has cancer."

All the beige in the room, the warm sunlight, the soft cushions that surrounded the sofas, failed to soften the blow of the doctor's words. Decor proved to be such an inadequate anesthetic.

"The disease has spread. I'm afraid we'll have to remove a number of her organs. We call it a Whipple procedure. It's quite common in these matters."

The chatter of the waiting room ceased, as though everyone, out of respect, agreed to put their own suffering on hold.

"What are you saying?" I asked.

"I'll need your permission to go forward with the operation. I went in there looking for something else. Now that we have this new development, I'll need the go-ahead from the family in order to proceed further. If you don't give it to me, I'll just close her back up and we can do this another time."

"What am I supposed to do? I can't make this decision. I'm not even old enough to vote yet!" My eyes were moist and scared, but the surgeon wasn't looking that deeply. "I don't want to gamble with my mother's life. It just doesn't seem right."

"As your mother's surgeon, I advise that you allow me to do the one thing in my power to save her. I think it's best that we do it now, but I will need your consent to do the operation. It's your call . . . unless of course you want to involve your father in this."

"No, I can't do that. . . . How are you with hearts?"

The surgeon looked at the clock on the wall as if to coax out of me a nerve that would give him his answer.

"What are the odds?" I asked, stalling for time.

"We're dealing with science and medicine here, son," he reminded me. "I'm afraid you have to take a chance. You'll make a decision and live with it. That's the best you can do."

The doctor left with his orders: the answer he desired. I remained in the corner of the room. My brain slowly readjusted to the surroundings. The buzz returned to the room. Pacers resumed their well-worn paths; magazine pages flipped back and forth mindlessly; arabesques of smoke, the exhaust of unending cigarettes, chased the ceilings.

Across the room I stared at my father, who seemed lost in his own solitary vigil. What to tell him? How much loss can a person endure?

I knew about those years in the concentration camp. The slaughter of his family; those months hiding in the forest, a marksman clinging to the tactical limbs of protective trees; the quest to begin anew in America. Then the debilitating heart attacks—one after another, relentless, like the rapid blasts from a rifle. And the episodic depressions. Those lifelong frailties, consuming what had not yet been completely worn out.

Longingly, I remembered the way he was when I was a small child, before the illness—solid, rough, mysterious, painfully silent. The refugee with the haunted past. A comic-book creation, like all those other tortured humans who had acquired extraordinary, but unwanted, powers. A freak accident of history had transformed him into a superman—without the cape, although shrouded nonetheless.

He would wrestle me on the carpet, the sounds of my laughter overwhelming his own entombed joy. The hair on his chest would prick my tender skin. I could feel the warmth of his quickened breath; hear the echoes of those still vibrant beats, the drumming of a lion's pulse . . . all before the arterial sabotage.

But that man went away, replaced by the afflicted creature whose life accelerated in tragic bursts of deterioration. Visits to the hospital; afraid of looking at him in that wheelchair, pretending that wasn't my father—couldn't be the same man, the one who could roll me over his back so easily, now reduced to the role of a condemned survivor. My childhood, tiptoeing around the house, being warned daily of his impending death. No rides hoisted upon the shoulders; no playing catch after school. It was a fatherless upbringing, and yet there was a father.

He must have noticed me speaking with the doctor, no doubt wondering what the surgeon had to say. What was I going to tell him? Explain the Whipple procedure? I wasn't even sure what it was.

"How you feeling, Dad?" I rested a hand on his shoulder—for me, and for him.

His mind must have been full, retracing his steps, marveling at his own endurance. The man had already outlived one wife. This past was never mentioned, certainly not in front of me. But I had decoded some whispers about an Elka—not a real relative—who was murdered by the Nazis. Now the second spouse, my mother, was succumbing to a biological enemy—but still the same consequence. Unaware of what was being prescribed for her, the kinds of incisions contemplated, the radical unearthings that were about to take place.

"Can I get you anything? They got a cafeteria down the hall. I bet they have apple pie. Your favorite."

He looked up at me with the eyes of a child who had lost its voice and its way—wanting to be picked up, carried out of the hospital, taken to a park, or for a scoop of vanilla. Reaching into his pocket, he removed a tiny bottle of nitroglycerin pills. He opened the top, scattered a few pellets into his palm, and consumed them in one shaky, unhesitating gulp. Over the years he had become adept at these swallowings, the easing of palpitations, the relief from the savage poundings.

"Everything's going to be okay," I said, wishing for my own pill. "Don't worry."

Two jittery hands—one withered, the other young but searching— reached into the wooden box and removed the mandatory skullcaps. Father and son were about to enter a house of Jewish worship, a place that routinely frowned on hatless entries. In the past they had shown little interest in making such pilgrimages, but circumstances always change. One must always bend with the times, and the dilemmas.

It was a small shul, wedged in between a hardware store and a bakery in the run-down section of Atlantic City. A one-story wooden building, painted pale blue on the outside with a fake mahogany wood interior. The Star of David above the front door rattled from its hinges. It tilted to one side and dipped a little forward, threatening to come crashing down on each unsuspecting, and godforsaken, supplicant. The sanctuary smelled of glue. Hard times had changed this neighborhood. The Jews had gone off to Florida and to other towns along the Jersey shore. The shul was now an outpost in case anybody wanted to return, a memorial to the rituals of the past, a place where Jewish gamblers could wander in search of a blessing that might change their luck.

The father was old. He moved slowly. His hair was still dark, but his face was worn and deeply wrinkled. The body was shrunken and unsteady. His eyes were a brilliant blue, but were squinting, although the day was without much sunlight. The boy was tall, but seemed uncomfortable with this advantage over his father. He loped behind the old man, slouching forward, his soft face aging with each step.

Hesitating as they entered the synagogue, so long since their last visit. Had there been even one other time since the bar mitzvah? They couldn't remember. Stumbling in, overcome by the feeling that before they even sat down they had already gone about everything all wrong.

Such transparent maneuverings. They wanted something from their god. A rush order, no less. A word or two with the wizard. But they weren't entirely sure how much time you had to put in first before God took your prayers seriously. Or whether he would ever take them seriously. Or what the whole point to this prayer business was, anyway. Too late to build up any spiritual equity; what they lacked most now was seniority, and sincerity.

The two had been walking just outside the synagogue, clearing their minds of weighty distractions when they noticed the outstretched arms of the menorah and the precarious Star of David. Wavering, then looking at each other for an instant, there was a tacit acknowledgment between the generations that some outside help in coping with this latest crisis might be useful. Perhaps this was as good a time as any to restore, or at least revisit, their vanished faith.

"Should we?" the son asked.

"Maybe, why not?" said the father cautiously. "What do we have to lose?"

Needing air, they had just left the hospital. The news about the wife and mother was not good. One was to become a widower, the other a partial orphan. They walked away from the hospital, retreating from the reality that awaited them there.

The sanctuary was dark. Empty. There were no scheduled services, yet they still held them, even without a minyan. An old man, a holdover from the neighborhood—not even a rabbi— might show up later that day to officiate. Father and son were too early. That was good. They wouldn't know the difference, any- way. Beggars. They moved through the aisle and slithered into the first row.

The son turned to the father and asked, "What do we do now?"

"I was going to ask you. It's a shame your bar mitzvah was in English, not Hebrew. The lessons might have been useful right now." They reached for prayer books, hoping to find there some clue, an instruction manual perhaps.

Before them, printed in dense pica, the muscular letters of the Hebrew alphabet—dashes and dots hovering above and below like protective escorts. Another language. Even worse than Latin, of which the father at least knew a little.

"Which way do you open these books again?" the son won- dered.

"You have it upside down. No, the other way."

"What about a prayer shawl?"

"If God is listening, he won't notice."

"What should we say?"

The old man turned his head slowly, and said, "All these years I haven't been a father to you—too sick to do any good," a slight curl of smile breaking through the grief, "now, all of a sudden— after such a day—you need me."

"Okay, I'll make something up and whisper it in English."

"I'll shout," said the father.

"What about your heart? Be careful."

"It's my heart that wants to do the shouting."

The ark remained closed, but a bottle of nitroglycerin was opened as a precaution. The father roared like a wounded lion. The son looked on, helpless, untrained in how to remove the thorn.

The odds of losing both parents, one after another, are low. But in Atlantic City, for those willing to lay down a bet, you can get a spread on anything. Suddenly, against all odds and still too young to enter a casino, I had become a betting man.

"I'm very worried about him there alone in that apartment," I said.

"He'll be fine," my guidance counselor advised me. "People lose their spouses all the time. They go on and live. Maybe he'll even remarry."

Fine? Live? Remarry? I pondered, with raised eyebrows.

I was away at prep school. He went about his life on the Jersey shore. This is what he wanted—for our lives to continue as they had before. But we both knew that was impossible.

Some weekends I would take the train down for a visit. We would walk the length of the boardwalk together—all so reminiscent of old times, minus the carnival memories. The boardwalk had been refurbished: each board replaced, the strip widened, the arcade vendors gone—retired, replaced by the concrete crest of hotels and the lavish casinos that now loomed large on the crowded horizon.

They expanded the size of the beach, dredging up new sand, giving the seagulls an improved view while gliding above dry land. The crowds were younger. The conventioneers were gone. They had joggers now—some pounding on a landscaped strip of hard sand; others bouncing on the boards.

He asked how school was going, and I would improvise a tale to satisfy him. Within weeks I had developed quite a talent for exaggeration, and he an equal facility for shrewd, undisguised translation. Each vainly trying to protect the other, all the while conscious of the well-meaning artifice.

"So school is good?"

"Yes, Dad, everything is fine."

"You should not neglect your studies. Nothing is more important."

"I know."

"I want for you to be happy. Windsor is a good school, better than what we have here."

"But maybe I should come home, be with you."

"Nonsense. You go back."

On the phone we would hang up by saying "I love you." Before her death this would have been an unheard-of sentimental exchange. But suddenly an altogether new pattern of relations evolved, as though we had just been introduced and had no past experience in saying good-bye—when in fact, we had been preparing ourselves all along.

I had decided to exploit these new feelings. A crack in the silence had revealed itself, and I was determined to bust clear through to the other side. Or, failing that, at least slip by unnoticed. I wanted to know more about what had happened to him during the war. It was always such an impenetrable secret—my parents, speaking in code, changing the passwords repeatedly, keeping me off the scent. And he was always so ill. There was never the occasion to catch them off guard, ask the big questions, holding out for something other than that familiar silence.

As a child I knew the sketchy exterior of their story—an off-the-rack synopsis, not any different from what could be gotten out of the public library, or a PBS documentary. But the actual details of his life—the real adventures, not the imagined horror—were beyond my grasp, and his inclination to tell. Perhaps now was the time. Catching him at a vulnerable moment. Father to son. Man to man. Heart to weakened heart.

With age, disability, and despair he had become a slow walker. It seemed as though one of his short, tedious strides carried him absolutely no place at all, the kind of feeling you get while looking down from an airplane: the slow passage of clouds, the anchored land below. My knees ached from all this halted motion. Meanwhile, he enjoyed his walk, lost in some meditation, his mind racing far ahead of our apparent crawl. His arms were folded behind his back, his head dropped as though taking inventory of the boards. I moved a few steps in front of him, backpedaled a bit, then stopped.

"Hey, you won't guess what this place is."

"Right here?"

"Yeah. Take a guess."

"I don't know," he said, twisting around, checking his whereabouts for the first time.

"Come on, try your luck, show me what you're made of," I said, dropping a clue.

"Let's see," he surveyed, "we have come here so many times, so much has happened on these boards . . . it could be anything."

"Think way back, one of the first times you brought me here—when I was first able to walk on my own."

A faint recognition, then the twinkle of a follow-up smile. "Aha, yes . . . yes, of course—I lost you on the boardwalk. *Ach*, how could I forget that? You were so little. And so many people. You disappeared in the crowd. You weren't so far away, really, but it felt like it. So scared. A little bird, crying against the railing. A lady was calming you down. Poor thing—both of you; she had no luck at all, and you, a red face, tears everywhere, like you had been in the water." He looked off out into the ocean. "Was it right here?"

"Yes, right over there," I said, pointing over to the side, where it all began.

"How can you be sure this is the place?"

"That's where the rifle arcade was, next to that big tree over there. When I got lost, I kept watching that tree. It was the only thing that wasn't moving and making noise. Funny how you remember certain things. You can't get them out of your mind. Everything else here has changed—torn down, except the tree."

"What else do you remember?"

"I remember what made you let go of my hand. Do you?"

"The shooting arcade . . . so long ago . . ." His mind was drifting, folds of skin settled in around his temples as he squinted the vanished arcade into focus.

"I can't believe we never talked about this," I said, holding back tears. "You know, there's stuff I always wanted to know about that day, but I was afraid to ask."

"Why don't you ask me now?"

"Can I? Has the moratorium worn off?"

"I don't know. We'll find out."

"Okay. Before the crowd pushed me, I saw what you did with that rifle. *Pow, pow, pow,*" caressing my own imaginary weapon, "everything went down, everything. That big fat guy couldn't believe it. Where did you learn to shoot like that?"

There was no response.

"Uncle Stanley said you were a partisan in the forest. That must have been the place. They didn't teach you about guns in gymnasium, right?"

I had only just inched over the threshold, but already he was decomposing, wilting—the Hyde mask taking shape, always the preferred costume.

"In America, I'm disabled. In Europe, I led a different life. That's all. Let's just leave it at that."

"No, I want to hear more. I remember that at first we just walked away from the man, but then you ran back. What did he say that made you let go of my hand?"

His steely eyes looked right through me, making me shudder, sending an order to turn back, abandon the search before the trail of mysteries spilled out into the open like a disturbed grave.

"Hard to explain," he said. "A bad habit learned during the war, a lasting reaction, I guess."

"That's not enough. I need to know more."

"You think you need to know." Pausing, dousing the urgency of my plea. "What must you know? Do you want to know whether

I ever killed someone? How will that change anything? What mystery will that answer?" He was visibly angry, contradicting the weakness and defeat I always saw in him.

"Your mother is still dead. Your childhood is still filled with silence. Fifteen years ago, somewhere around here, they gave me a stuffed animal for shooting plastic ducks. A few years before I shot at human animals. There were no prizes for such killings. Such a strange world. A jungle. A circus.

"Nothing I tell you will change the fact that I could never have been a normal father. I came to you with a heart filled with loss. Not the best credentials for a parent. Maybe I had no right to have a child in the first place. I should never have let go of your hand. A very bad beginning. My first failure as your father. I was lost, and then I gave it to you."

I panicked. How to shut the spigot on this stream? "Hey, don't worry about it." Then reaching for his hand. "I'm still here. See? Right where you left me—just about the same spot."

"I see . . . now that I've found you after all these years, it's too late—you're a grown man."

The son lifted the receiver and was surprised by what he heard.

"I've decided to accept an invitation to a wedding," the father announced, "Hardoff's son, you know, Billy, the gym teacher. It's so soon after the funeral, yes, but I think it will do me good. What do you think?"

The son felt relieved. The mother's death had left both father and son unsure of the proper reentry points back into the orbit of life. The father struck first, the braver of the two. "Fine by me. I think you should go. You're not asking my permission, are you?"

"No, but I would like a favor."

"What is it?"

"I noticed in your room, you have hanging in the closet a pair of black velvet pants. You didn't take them up to school."

"Yeah, I know which ones they are."

"I would like to wear them. Could I? I have already tried them on—they fit."

"Of course," the son said, feeling his own joy at the father's renewed vigor. "A wedding, huh?"

"Yes, it is along the strip, at the ballroom of one of the casinos."

"Well . . . I guess . . . have fun!"

"I'll do the best I can. I'll call you tomorrow."

"Wait a minute. . . . They really fit?"

"Like a glove. Soon I will be too small for your clothes."

The next day there was no phone call. The son began to worry.

"He's dead," he predicted. "No one is picking up the phone." Then, flatly, quietly, "I can't believe it—my father's dead."

His roommates tried to persuade him otherwise.

"He's just out for the day. Relax."

He knew.

"First he had a wedding, now he's found something else to do. Your father's more cool than you are—just face it."

He knew.

"Both your parents can't die so close together. It just doesn't happen that way."

He knew.

At the end of the day, the police telephoned the school's dormitory. The father's body had been found on the boardwalk—a heart attack. They didn't know when it had happened. Morning joggers had found him facedown against the boards, hands raised up, surrendering to the sea.

The son packed hurriedly and, like the lost swell of a whitecap, returned to the Jersey shore. The black velvet pants were stretched out smooth on his bed when he arrived. For whom were they waiting? He wondered whether his father had gone to the wedding after all. Had he worn the pants? Did he die in them?

Walking along the boardwalk, wearing the same trousers, the son blended into the thickening afternoon crowd. When he arrived at the familiar tree, he stopped, not sure of where to go from there. The sun was setting on the other side of the hotels. Golden light filtered through the glass and warmed his face. His fingers fell into the soft velvet of the back pocket. A bottle of nitroglycerin, stuffed full with tablets, found his reaching hand. The final prize of the carnival.

AN
ACT OF
DEFIANCE

He announced his arrival with the resonance of a biblical deliverer.

"Adam, this is Haskell, your uncle, from Belgium. I come to New York in three weeks. I stay by you, no? We get to know each other. I fix your life."

The answering machine absorbed these words as though the machine and my uncle had been on speaking terms for years. "I fix your life," it had recorded. Maybe the machine knew what he meant. I sure didn't.

I pondered the message for a moment and concluded one thing: I wasn't at all prepared for his visit. The timing was awful. The semester would almost be over by then, and I would have many papers to grade. As the conniving provocateur of maturing minds that I am, I find it useful to absorb myself in my students' thoughts, those ersatz journals maintained throughout the semester for my class. Imagine asking city college kids to reflect on the horrors of the Holocaust. Most of them aren't even Jewish. Better to have them share lunar speculations than to ask the impossible.

I'd been teaching a humanities course on the Holocaust for ten years, and with each year—as the crime grew more distant, and the university's curriculum more eclectic—the reasons for its study seemed to lose urgency. Enrollment has been progressively down. Few considered graduate study; I couldn't even find a decent teaching assistant. Who was I kidding? It was a miracle when my undergraduates indulged me by staying awake. And who could blame them? History, like fashion, has its trends. "The Holocaust in the Modern World" was an apparent misnomer—the academic equivalent of bell-bottoms and platform shoes. Even my colleagues, who had long since moved on to bioethics and the menace of the nuclear age, began looking at me a little funny, as though I, alone among the faculty, had been wearing my underwear on my head all along.

So what was I to expect from those journals, anyway? The wisdom and conceits of my students? The satisfaction of my own curiosities?

Haskell's visit was bound to interrupt my concentration; his own history so incomparable, so incompatible with that idle mush of plagiarized words—the very best that my students could manage. One would need time to prepare for such a visit. It wasn't simply a matter of smoothing out a pullout couch, or buying extra orange juice, or getting tickets to a Broadway show. This was no ordinary man. All my resources would have to be recruited into the service of looking after an old survivor of the Holocaust. Normally my appetite for *Shoah* nostalgia would have lusted for the challenge that a man of Haskell's background could offer. But not now. I felt certain that, at this particular time, the journals, the exams, and my uncle's complementary presence was too much—a Holocaust overdose with fatal consequences.

This Uncle Haskell, never before seen in my life, was my last surviving relative. He had crawled out from Auschwitz with dysentery, typhus, and an assortment of other infirmities that would have entitled him to a lifetime of unbroken animus. Now, nearing eighty, he was a walking ghost of horrors past. I imagined what he looked like, this witness who wouldn't go away, this author of all that silent testimony.

But never having seen him before, how did I know?

Because I wanted to see him that way. I insisted. Until we were to meet face-to-face, my imagination took control of our introduction, our fraternity, our good-byes. This was my way with his ilk. Yet another in a long series of mangled family portraits, constructed by me, for me. The same was done with my parents, no longer alive but continually reinvented, revised, hostage to my own private therapy. The Holocaust survivor as myth, as fairy tale, as bedtime story. I had created my own ghosts from memories that were not mine. I wasn't there, in Poland, among the true martyrs. Everything about my rage was borrowed. My imagination had done all the work—invented suffering, without the physical scars, the incontestable proof.

Trapped inside a doctoral thesis that has guided my adult life. *Descent into Darkness*—an academic title, a personal mantra. Suffocating among all those images. The indignant fingers pointing like daggers in all directions. The reciting of ordered statistics; the sharing of survivor testimonies. How to relieve myself of the burdens, the obligations? Plotting my escape from the scholarship, and the legacy. Away from all those meticulous references to camps and crematoriums. Slinking back into an imperfect but amiable world where children play on rusty swings, the sweet hum of their laughter, the background music to their innocence.

But Haskell would only extend the torment. He was the real thing, on his way to supply me with a quick fix, to feed my guilt, replenish my craving for the soul of survivors. He was all that was left of the family elders. The only one who could recollect the nightmare—offering the right mix of family tenderness and trauma.

As is my practice, I insist on meeting guests at the airport. To the uninitiated and the first-time visitor, New York resembles a city under siege. Clamorous jostling for position everywhere. Individuals scatter madly, proving their worthiness as contestants in the mindless chase. As one arrives by air, the first sightings are epic. Once on the ground, however, there is cause for retreat everywhere. It is as uninviting as one could imagine.

But my hospitality requires some patience. Because the Nazis, as a people, prided themselves on punctuality, I, as an individual, revel in tardiness. My students at Hunter College, where I teach that generally undersubscribed seminar, know that my fidelity to the college's schedule is predictably nonexistent. On such solemn occasions as the syllabus inspires, my students saunter in quietly, heads dropped in plaintive respect, but late—always late, in keeping with my example, the mood I inflict.

"What do we know about the Germans?" I ask rhetorically on the first day of class each year—ten minutes behind schedule. "They made the trains run on time. Everyone knows that. So what does that tell us about civilization, about precision, about order? Are these enviable values, if so easily corrupted to kill innocent people? During the semester you will read what one writer, Theodor Adorno, had to say on the subject. He tried to reconcile the making of art after the Holocaust. He said 'After Auschwitz there is no more poetry.' So I borrow a little from Mr. Adorno and say: 'After Auschwitz, clocks no longer have hands.' Time is meaningless, it is the plaything of barbarians."

I hold up both wrists in demonstration. "You see, I don't even wear a watch. So come to class, but don't expect to find me here on time. I don't wish to honor the obsessions of murderers with my timely presence."

The stage has been set, my performance effective, but alienating. This is no ordinary class. The teacher is not suitably objective. What kind of prelude to learning is this? Some angrily consult the course catalogue, searching for deceit in the description. Others simply pray for alternate electives during the same time slot.

On the day that Haskell was to arrive in New York, I was sitting nervously in the backseat of a taxi, surrounded by a commune of other cabs all stalled amidst choking vapors. A streak of sun shot through the window and warmed the lap of my blue jeans. Even without a watch, I knew that Haskell's plane had already landed. Fortunately, knowing my penchant for lateness, I had called ahead and asked Sabena to inform Uncle Haskell that I was on the way and not to worry.

I had this picture in my mind of Haskell at U.S. Customs: he was being asked to show his passport.

"Papers, sir!"

"What . . . I . . ."

He fumbles excitedly. Nervous beyond sedation. A Jew with ethnically incriminating papers and a convenient scarlet letter—the shape of a Star of David—patched onto his lapel. Hands move in and out of pockets. A mad search. Sweat builds on his forehead, then plunges into his eyes. The customs agent grows impatient. He is a man with a large face and thick eyelids that refuse to blink; the steely resolve of a bureaucrat dedicated to the rules. His nose is heavily diagrammed with blood vessels, like the map of a congested autobahn. Fingers tap away on a white Formica counter.

"Sir, I must see your papers! Now . . . Jew!"

In unconscious rescue of a fallen uncle, I screamed from the backseat of the cab, "Stop!"

"Where? Here?" the driver, a Turk, said. "Mister, we are almost stopped in this traffic. If you want to get out, fine, but where would you go on the Grand Central?"

"Sorry, never mind," I said, recovering, rolling down the window in a furious and desperate exchange of air.

"Just let him go," I repeated to myself, still conjuring the image of my uncle at the airport. "Hasn't the man already suffered enough?"

The vision, and the traffic, disappeared, each dissolving like clouds into a vast horizon. We picked up speed and Kennedy Airport was before us.

"Quickly, the Sabena arrival gate," I said.

My fears and suspicions were well justified. There was an ambulance and two earnest-looking attendants wheeling a stretcher through noisy mechanical doors. *Aha*, my intuition about Customs was right, I thought. Working from a gut sense of family resemblance, it looked as though a relative of mine was being loaded into the ambulance.

In haste, I paid the cab driver—slipping him an inadvertent twenty-dollar tip—and rushed over. As the stretcher rolled on its path, I saw the face of a beaten man, glassy tubes dangling from his nose, wisps of unswept hair. Amidst the commotion, a tap upon my right shoulder caused me to turn around just as the ambulance sped away.

"Adam, this is you? You look just like your father."

It was Uncle Haskell, standing before me, not a discernible scratch on him.

"Thank God you're safe," I said, placing my hands on his shoulders, keeping an arm's-length distance. "I thought that man in the ambulance was you."

A big smile seemed painted on Haskell's face, which faded, only for a moment. "Poor man. I saw him fall down. Too much baggage he was carrying. A man of his age. He needed help. I was about to assist him, but then it was too late."

He was going to help the old man? How could that be? Standing next to Haskell were four oversized trunks, arranged side by side like enormous domino tiles. How did *he* manage to drag these boulders all the way from Belgium to New York, I wondered, and how long was he planning to stay?

There was a familiarity to his face—high forehead, prominent nose, powder blue eyes, ears protruding from his head in a decided flare. He didn't look that much unlike my father at that age, or some of my other now-departed relatives from the Posner clan. Haskell was the last one. The lone survivor. The passer of the torch. And then there was me, filled with fear of a fumble.

"I was worried that it was you, Uncle Haskell. I came running."

"Why were you running? And what could you do if it was me? A man of my age makes peace with death. There is nothing to fear anymore. You worry too much, Adam. Your father told me about you—too serious, brooding, not able to enjoy life."

"My father said that? He should talk. Where do you think I learned it from?"

"He was concerned about you. That's why I am here. Your father had an excuse for his suffering. What reason do you have to carry these sins around like bricks?"

"I have no choice," I said assuredly. "It's called legacy. The

Holocaust survivor in me was passed on through the genes. Who knows how many generations it will take to cancel this virus from our blood?"

We stood motionless outside the airport. Fumes clouded the air. In this suspended silence, I began to feel bad about my terse handling of Haskell's guidance. How could my gloom compare with his, no matter how practiced I had become at it? Me, Adam Posner, unharmed in New York, never the victim of even a veiled anti-Semitic remark, an entire ocean and a full generation removed from the ghettos and the camps. My DNA may be forever coded with the filmy stuff of damaged offspring, the handicap of an unwanted inheritance. But perhaps Uncle Haskell wasn't the most sympathetic audience for this kind of self-indulgent reverie.

He tilted his head to the side, taking measure of his nephew.

As the silence mounted and our eyes looked for something else to do, I noticed that Haskell still had a full head of hair. This surprised me: a man of his age and a recipient of our family's heredity. My own hair had thinned to oblivion, and my father's head, by the time he had reached Haskell's age, was a complete wasteland of shiny skin, devoid of any life-form. Somehow Haskell had escaped our family's predicament—at least with regard to his head.

Finally I decided to hail a cab, and with the compassion of a good citizen, I assisted the driver in storing in the trunk of the car what must have been all of Haskell's worldly possessions. On the road, heading toward Manhattan, I asked Haskell how long he planned on staying.

"When my work is through."

"What work is that?"

"You'll see."

Despite his advanced age, Haskell had developed an immunity to jet lag. Before putting any of his things away, he announced: "I must go out."

"What? Uncle, it's late, almost nine o'clock. You just got in. And where are you going?"

"May I use your phone?"

"Sure, but . . ."

He was in the next room. The muted tones of an elderly man filled the apartment, a shadowy accent that defied translation.

He returned and said: "Okay, now I go."

"Can I go with you?"

"No, I go alone."

"Can't it wait till tomorrow?"

"No."

"Do you know where you're going? How to get a cab? The subway? For god's sakes, don't take the subway at this hour. Please, don't go."

So he left me with his unpacked luggage, which dominated the living room like barricades. This mysterious visit, from the outset, was gaining in intrigue. Haskell was guarded in his actions, as well as in his words. Hours passed as I stood watch, like an anxious father waiting for the return of a curfew-mocking child. Finally, well past midnight, Uncle Haskell returned, or I should I say, stumbled in.

"Nephew! My boy! Such a nice city have you here—the pretty lights, the loud noises, the many people," he said, his words slurring into one another, adding a new level of difficulty to our visit. Then he started to sing. " 'New York. New York. Such a wonderful town.' The Bronx is there and the Battery," he paused, laughing, ". . . is also there."

He shut the door forcefully, then opened his arms, giving me a spirited hug.

"Where have you been?" I asked coldly. An involuntary twitch in my shoulder was the only sound in an otherwise still apartment. "You've been worrying me again."

"I see that with you there is no other choice," he replied, barely taking notice of the scowl on my concerned face. He paraded around the apartment, opening up his luggage and finding places for each article inside.

"Well, where were you?"

"On a date."

"On a date?"

"That's correct."

"With whom?"

"A lady I met in Antwerp last summer. She works in the diamond business. She has a shop here in New York, off Forty-seventh Street."

"You came all the way from Brussels to go on a date? I thought you were coming to see me—to 'fix my life,' whatever that means. I was looking forward to hearing stories about your life—the ghetto, the camp, the relocation center."

Haskell frowned, and said, "Nephew. I should come here, all the way from Belgium, to talk about the camps? This you need? I am afraid your head is already too much filled with stories about the camps."

He surveyed the room, his head turning in all directions. Everywhere he was surrounded by bookshelves, not an empty space to be found—not even for a simple magazine. I had devoted my life to the study of his wartime tribulations. Books that he had neither heard of nor read welcomed my uncle. The historians, philosophers, the psychologists, the theologians, the novelists, the poets, the playwrights—all had appropriated the Holocaust, making the suffering universal—"man's inhumanity to man"—the wail and shriek of the twentieth century. A cottage industry of Holocaust speculation had risen from the ashes of the dead, a fittingly smug reversal of those Nazi bonfires.

Shrinking against the magnitude of it all—the sum and substance of the *Shoah* consolidated into the living room of a one-bedroom New York apartment—he said, "As I look around this room, I see that you have dedicated yourself well to the study of what happened to us. But what has this all done to you?"

He walked over to a shelf: Dawidowicz, Wiesel, Levi, Donat, Hilberg, Ringelblum, Bauer—all stared at him, monastically, in shared fraternal recognition of his suffering. All it took was a knowing nod.

"All I'm saying is that I am anxious to hear you tell me your life story," I repeated.

"And I am anxious to get to know you. There is a difference in what we seek."

"But you just got here. You didn't have any time to settle in yet, and then you were off. And now you smell from liquor," I said disapprovingly.

"What is so wrong with my having the companionship of a woman? And why should I not drink? I am alive. Death have I seen. From death I have escaped. I have no more interest in what it holds for me. I celebrate life instead. Even at my age, life is filled with women, and drink, and dance."

"As a way to forget?"

"Not to forget; to remember—to be of this world. I can't forget what happened to me, our family, our people. But I will not shut myself from the world either. With this your father would not agree. I still know survivors who carry on this way, like your father did. Silent suffering. A private death that traveled with him, wherever he went, a ghost always on his shoulder, whispering into his ear, not letting him eat, work, rest. We spoke many times about this. I would say, 'I survived the camps in order to live. To be like you, marchers in the army of the living dead, is a victory for the Nazis. They wanted to kill us all, and they failed. I won't give them the satisfaction by living an unhappy life.' You see, Adam, my life, with all the riches and pleasures that I allow myself, is an act of defiance. I am an assassin to their mission. So I drink. I live. Don't worry, I too flirt with my demons, just like your father. I just don't show it. Enemies grow strong when they recognize fear in the eyes of their victims. Remember that. Now, where do I sleep?"

"Over there," I said, pointing to a pullout sofa on which already rested much of Haskell's unpacked belongings.

"Ah, yes," he said with a devilish smile, "a bed in disguise. So right for me, no?"

"I don't know, is it?"

He didn't answer.

"One final thing, Adam," he remarked, holding onto a pair of slippers and a bathrobe. "You know about my condition, don't you? I'm sure your father told you? I need to spend a lot of time in the bathroom. I have to irrigate myself. Clean myself out."

The memory returned to me like a dream long since frozen in time. I did know. After the war, Haskell had been very sick. Through all those operations, he was left with a colostomy bag for a bowel. "His *tuchas* no longer works," my father would say in describing his Belgian brother.

Clean myself out. I will always remember those words; the organic imperative that it suggested, the dignity with which he refused to part.

"Yes, I know, Uncle."

"I hope it won't be too much trouble for you. I take a long time in the bathroom—for the irrigation."

"It won't be a problem," I assured him.

"Good. Now we sleep," he announced.

His eyes seemed weary from the long journey that brought him from Brussels to my apartment—in less than a day. I wanted to know more about his planned visit: why was he here, how long was he planning to stay, and how did I fit in. But I would have to wait. He shuffled into the bathroom. Irrigation and cleansing called.

The next morning I awoke to find Haskell gone. The foldout bed was made, hidden from sight, slipped back into the belly of the sofa. There was no evidence of his arrival the day before. Even his suitcases were tucked away someplace, or perhaps he had taken them with him, to his next destination.

My uncle was not who I had imagined. He was playing a role so out of character for the man he was. But was he playing? All these years of conjuring up ghosts, hoarding shadowy images of the anguished survivor, only now to find myself suitably stumped—betrayed by one of my own family, no less. Nowhere was his paradigm to be found among my accumulated archives. His suffering was elsewhere; set aside, like his luggage. Even with a colostomy bag dragging from behind, he made dashing exits—a Jewish James Bond, a tightless Robin Hood.

Admittedly, I had been spoiled in these pursuits. My father and his refugee friends were such willing and good-natured accomplices; so naturally they satiated my need to commune with the martyr. Long-suffering and forever brooding. Punished by inhumanity, indifference; a century that had fallen asleep; a godless world, or perhaps, too much God, not enough man. Life had disappointed my father, and in return, he chose to punish it by refusing any happiness that it might one day offer. How much he miscalculated: life would show so little distress in the face of his sacrifice.

Resting on the dining table, propped up without the aid of a mannequin, was a full head of hair—Haskell's hair. What the day before I believed to be an ancestral aberration was, in fact, unnatural to his head. Erect, full of wavy strands, it was more helmet than hairpiece, a cowl of charcoal gray.

My attention turned from the toupee to a note on the table:

Adam:

I hope you slept well. I left early. My habit in Belgium. I go to visit today some survivor friends who live in Brooklyn. My hair I leave to you because without it they would not know or remember me, if I came to them like this. They know the shaved head, and I do not want to disappoint. For them, they are still trapped in the world of your father. They lost their hair, and their strength, many years ago. From your writings, which I read last night (sorry I didn't ask first, but you were sleeping), I see I have much work to do to help my nephew. There is *tsouris* everywhere my boy, but there is always more if this is all you see.

I now go to visit friends, and I leave you my hair—for strength, like it gives me.

See you tonight.

Uncle Haskell

P.S. I would like to go to Atlantic City. You should come with me. We go later. Get to know each other. Rendezvous at six. Your flat.

He left me his hair. This for my troubles. As a second-rate substitute for meaningful dialogue, he treated me to an interview with his vanity.

I have remained a bachelor all my adult life. Never once have I been intrigued by the voices that swirl about a filled room. I don't need company. I'm not much for mingling—not sure I even know what it means. And yet somehow, after reading Haskell's note, I was overcome by a wicked loneliness. The feeling was actually foreign to me, like a new ailment I had discovered. There among my possessions, surrounded by the drab, lifeless decor of a sullen academic, the solace of familiar furniture—all that which normally offers me the cradle of home—and yet now, it all seemed so unsatisfying, so remote, strange even. With this profound sense of displacement, the balancing of alien impulses, I couldn't help but wonder who was visiting whom.

To what insidious game of cat and mouse was I becoming an unwilling player?

"The man is eighty!" I ruminated, pacing around my apartment. "He travels across the Atlantic, presumably to see me, and when he gets here, he avoids me like the plague."

So much time devoted to understanding the interior world of these people, their rhythms, their unnatural ways, the complex machinery that prevailed over the grandest Darwinian experiment of all. Had I finally lost patience for it all? I had been sitting with the Holocaust too long. Perhaps it was time to rest, try a new obsession, a hobby, perhaps. If Haskell had set out to reorient my ways, he was succeeding without even messing his hair.

It was late April. The spring semester was soon to be over. Without a coat, I left the apartment hurriedly, grabbing a stack of journals to grade. There were a few more lectures for me to prepare and deliver before the end of the term, but the journals, as

always, preceded the final exam. Yellow-and-white spiral note-
books had been turned into my office, piled high, filled with a mixed
bag of earnest confessions and worthless drivel, and occasionally
a discerning observation from a student whose mind was up to the
material.

I hid in Central Park, sitting on a bench near Belvedere Castle. There were pigeons surrounding my feet, although I had nothing to offer them. One had already left a blotchy memento of
white right beside me on the bench. Over by the Great Lawn, dogs
were chasing one another, their owners, standing off near the
Delacorte Theater, leashes in hand, busily engaged in the rival-
rous patter of the Upper West Side. I was seated alone with my
shadows, immersed in the calm, unconflicted reflections of my
students. The Holocaust as a mere course, an elective, and not
an obsession.

On and on I read:

> Killing has become too easy. People kill all the time. What's
> the difference between the Holocaust and a regular mur-
> der? A guy who works in a convenience store in my par-
> ents' neighborhood was killed just the other day.

I try to restrain myself in my comments, which straddle the mar-
gins of the page, ready to attack at the slightest provocation. "As
far as I am aware, people who work in 7-Elevens, although em-
ployed in a dangerous workplace, are not an endangered species.
They have not been 'selected for extermination' by the govern-
ment. The killings in this instance are random, a function of eco-
nomic, and socioeconomic, crime. And of course, you can always
change jobs, do something else for a living; but a Jew is a Jew. For
them, there was no escape."

> Black people were slaves in this country, but there aren't
> any humanities courses about that. How come? We could
> look at why people make slaves of one another. But no one

seems to want to talk about that, and how that's all related to the larger question of racism. The point is, when something bad happens to a Jew, everybody's got to hear about it. The Jews have all the power.

I reply: "From your mouth to God's ear. All that 'power' hasn't really protected Jews very much from persecution, no matter where they lived. And also, I think you're right; we should offer a humanities course on racism."

There is no god. God is dead. We killed God. There is no hope. We should just keep killing until we kill ourselves all up. . . .

No idea how to respond here. Very disturbed student. Why my class?

There was a chill in the air. Dappled light flickered on my students' pages. Across from me a woman stared intently at a picture of a small child. Her face grew tender as though the child was about to appear and put an end to the longing.

Hours passed without my paying much attention. I had graded all I could read. I was drowning in a pool of silent screams, which had nothing to do with what I had been reading.

Finally, from a distance I saw Haskell making his way toward me. I had left him a note, telling him where I'd be. But I never expected that he would set out to find me. I even warned him not to come. This is Central Park. No place for a man of his age, certainly not one who wasn't from New York and who wouldn't know to be aware of the inviting turns off the main road that could lead to danger. Besides, the park is so big. Even with directions, how could he track me down?

His shape grew clearer with each step, a rounding of features, a counting off of dimensions. By the time he reached me, we both stood amidst the dim western light that bathed the walls of the castle.

"Nephew, how are you?" he said, offering me his hand. The hand was cold.

"Fine," I replied. "Just finishing up grading papers. How did you find me?"

"I walked into the park and asked where the castle is. Some nice people sent me here." He then looked up at the stone walls, the arching steps, and remarked: "Very nice building. Who lives here? Donald Trump?"

"No, nobody lives here," I said, harshly.

"What's bothering you, Adam? You don't like that I should come here?"

"Uncle, you can't just walk into Central Park, at the end of the day—someone your age, no less—and ask strangers where to find your nephew. It just isn't done. It's too dangerous. You could have gotten mugged."

"Mugged. Don't be silly. Me? Mugged?" he started to laugh out loud like an old kook. "You sound like a tourist, Adam. Central Park is safe." He looked around, admiring the urban vista: the rolling hills, the thick trees, the colorful blur of Rollerbladers and streaking cyclists. "Why must you be so this way? This is a beautiful park. What are you seeing?"

"Look, I live here, you don't. I know what kinds of things go on in this park."

"Any sexual things? I like sex."

"Stop it! You're kidding me, right?"

He looked at me blankly, then continued: "You must be angry with me . . . because I left so early this morning. Is that it?"

"I'm not angry. Let's go home."

"No, I want to stay. Such a nice park. It is still early. So many people here, all here after work. Do you have a bicycle at home?"

"No."

"You live so close to this park, and you have no bicycle. What kind of boy are you?"

"Uncle, I'm forty years old. I haven't been on a bicycle in years."

"Nonsense. No one is too old for a bicycle. I have a bicycle in

Belgium. I want to go for a ride here in this park, with all these people."

"Uncle, I don't think I even know how to ride a bicycle anymore."

"This too doesn't surprise me. Come, I'll show you."

We walked over to the east side of the park. Haskell was unable to take his eyes off of a few tall, long-legged women who were running along the path of the Great Lawn. We headed a little south, past Cleopatra's Needle and the Metropolitan Museum of Art, over toward the boat pond. One of my students once told me that a man rented bicycles there. He was right. An elderly Italian gentlemen with a thick mustache was busy racking bicycles as we approached.

"Do you rent bicycles?" I asked.

"Yes," he replied. "How many you like?"

"One," Haskell said.

"One?" I turned to him and asked, "You don't want me to ride with you, now? Are we going to spend any time together on this trip?"

I was beginning to wonder whether Haskell saw the bicycle as a faster way to pick up women, and he feared that having me around would only set his efforts back somewhat.

"No, we go together. We would like that one," he said, pointing over to a separate stack in the corner.

"Oh, you want a tandem," the vendor said.

"Yes, a bicycle for two." Haskell smiled, showing the gaps between his teeth, and making a peace sign with his fingers.

The man rolled the bicycle out to us, and Haskell said immediately, "I'll go to the front."

"I think it would be better if I lead. I know the park."

"I'm the better driver," he said. "You watch me."

He straddled the front end of the tandem, which was red and a bit beat-up. There was a rust-covered RENT ME license plate dangling from my backseat.

"Hold on, nephew, here we go!"

Haskell navigated the bicycle ably, keeping it steady as we headed north on the east side of Central Park, up the first big hill. I was grossly out of shape. Up the hill my breath turned into a wheezing cough.

"Books are not so good for your health, no?" he said, tilting his head back at me. "Excuse me," he said politely to a lone jogger, waving his arms as if to shoo the runner away. Coming down the hill, he removed his feet from the pedals and, stretched out like a wishbone, allowed them to dangle from his sides. " 'New York, New York . . .' " he began to sing.

Haskell rang the bell several times as a warning to other cyclists, Rollerbladers, and pedestrians that the Posner boys were on the loose. But even when the road was clear, Haskell continued to ring the bell. He seemed to like the way it sounded.

"Now *this* is a good time," he said, taking his hands off the handlebars for a moment, raising his arms to the sky, and laughing like a madman.

"Uncle, please, be careful."

A cool wind smacked against my face, and what was left of my thinning hair was caught firmly in the breeze. Haskell's head of synthetic hair didn't budge. It remained still and groomed, as if it were plastered on. He said that he had bicycled often in Belgium. Perhaps the toupee was designed for such gusty adventures.

Up and down the hills we pedaled, speeding faster along the straightaway, near the reservoir. I didn't say anything, because a part of me feared for our safety—and I wasn't particularly good at acknowledging delight, anyway—but I soon settled into the ride, and was beginning to enjoy myself. It was a different way to see the park, to spend the afternoon, to live in New York.

As we pressed on, toward the 102nd Street traverse, I saw a young woman, her blond hair stuffed underneath a Styrofoam helmet, fall from her bicycle. Another cyclist had swerved into her lane, cutting her off. She didn't appear hurt, just a big long scrape along her knee. But as she was about to retrieve her bike, a teenager ran over from the other side of the road, lifted the bicycle, straddled it, and began to ride away.

"Hey, come back here!" she yelled.

"Did you see that, Uncle?"

"Yes. Let's go after him," he said.

All I could say was, "Why not?"

And we pedaled faster, watching as the boy turned west through the traverse over to the other side of the park. Because the stolen bicycle had pedals made for special shoes, the boy wasn't getting very far. His swollen basketball sneakers were spinning away vainly and awkwardly.

"We almost got him!" I said. "Keep pedaling, Uncle! Stay close, we're almost there!"

The kind of moment I always long for. Righting an injustice. Championing the oppressed. Fighting off the bully. Second nature called, urging me forward, as though my father's ghost lurked somewhere in the trees at the north end of Central Park.

As we pulled up beside the boy, who was breathing nervously, pedaling as fast as he could go, looking straight ahead, Haskell said, "Time to stop, boy. Off the bicycle!"

The boy refused to even look our way. I alertly grabbed the collar of his jacket, let go of my handlebars, and started to drag his bicycle, and our tandem, down to the ground. The bicycles swerved and we all fell down an embankment, onto a soft landing by some trees.

I got to my feet quickly, picked the teenager up, and pushed him against a tree.

"Tough guy, huh?" I said. "Stealing bicycles from girls in Central Park?"

Haskell got up slowly, dusted himself off, then realized that both his hair, and his colostomy bag, had become undone. Before he began to put himself back together, he walked over to where I was. I was busy squeezing the teenager's arms, holding him forcefully against the tree.

"Leave the boy alone, Adam," Haskell said. "He is not a Nazi. Just a boy. Put an end to the fight in you, please. There is no shame."

"This kind of thing leads to other Holocausts, Uncle!" I said. "I'm going to teach him a lesson."

"This is what a humanities professor understands as the Holocaust? This is what is in those books?"

I looked into the boy's face. He wasn't old enough to shave and he was trembling. I should let him go. What had he stolen, after all? Just a bicycle. But then, isn't that how they all start out? Smash a few windows, break some glass. What kind of beast might he one day turn into? Nazis were once boys, don't forget. Let me put an end to someone else's future suffering. . . .

"Let him go, Adam."

I cooled off and released the kid. "Get out of here," I said.

He ran off into the trees, looking back behind him, making sure that we weren't about to chase him again.

"You have much in common with your father—more than you will ever know."

We picked up the young woman's bicycle and returned it to her. She was still waiting on the east side of the park, hoping to flag down a policeman. Grateful, but still a little shaken. As for our means of transportation, my stunt had completely twisted the tandem beyond repair. The bicycle was now unridable.

"Sorry, Uncle. I know you were having a good time."

"Not to worry. Big park, much more to do."

We returned the tandem to the man back at the boat pond.

"I should never have rented to you two in the first place. Your friend is too old, and you look crazy to me," he said, shaking his head, wondering how he would ever get the bicycle back in working order.

Haskell hadn't had his fill of Central Park. As we walked a little further south, he noticed a merry-go-round.

"Ah, this I like."

He paid for three rides, the oldest man by far to ride that week.

Smiling at the little children, making faces at me, laughing in tune with the fairground music.

On his last ride, he made sure that I mounted a horse right beside him. The Posners took a spin around the park, after all.

When Haskell was finally through with the merry-go-round, as the twilight set in and the headlights from commuting taxis circled past us, he said, "I have an idea for tonight and tomorrow."

"What now?"

"We go to Atlantic City."

I shook my head, my eyes lost focus. "There's gambling in Atlantic City, Uncle."

"I know this. It's legal, no?"

"Yes, but why would you want to go there?"

"Many lights, beautiful women—I hear you can drink for nothing as long as you gamble. That's good. Also, I see here that Tom Jones will be singing tonight at Caesars," he said, pulling out a glossy brochure that he had apparently picked up on his travels in Manhattan. "I like him very much. 'What's new pussycat, wo oh wo oh wo oh,' " he started singing. "Why should we not go?"

"Don't you ever get tired? Not enough excitement today? We should have been getting an early-bird special somewhere, with a senior citizen's discount, no less; but instead we have this action-packed afternoon in Central Park. Why couldn't we have just gone home to talk? I want to know things, things about your life. You don't want to talk. You don't even want to go home and watch PBS. You're not like most older people, are you?"

Haskell looked at me lovingly. He was trying to reach me, but in a different way from what I wanted, from what I thought I needed—the only way I knew.

The whole thing was so preposterous. To go off to Atlantic City with this deranged uncle of mine. We hadn't even had dinner yet. Shoot craps, hear Tom Jones. Neither would have much bearing on the college's tenure decision.

"So, Professor Posner, we hear you were in Atlantic City, corrupting the morals of a senior citizen."

And what kind of a visit was this? So much for my continued enlightenment about the *Shoah*.

"So we go?" Haskell persisted.

"Yes, we go."

Within minutes, Haskell had me back at the apartment. He rummaged through a valise, his hand feeling through a sewn-in compartment, removing a stash of currency. "We need this to lay down our bets," he announced authoritatively, as though his book-ish nephew was completely unaware as to how one participates in a casino. "Now I must check to see that on my hair is on tight, and then we go."

Next stop, the subway at Eighty-sixth Street and Broadway. We needed to get downtown to the Port Authority, where we would then board the line to Atlantic City. As we waited for the subway to arrive, a man, standing on the platform, was singing. His only musical accompaniment was a string attached to an overturned washbasin, which he played with all the soulfulness of a bass. At moments when the tracks were silent, when the local held back and the express was nowhere in sight, the man's sweet jazz riff echoed down below, in the entombed chamber of mass transit. He was singing "Only Fools Rush In." Haskell's face beamed with each harmonic note. Beneath the smile a foot was tapping, keep-ing time to what was for him an uncommon musical idiom. He reached into his pocket and removed some change, walking over to drop some inside the crooner's hat.

The busker nodded in appreciation, his fingers plucking at the string. "Good evening, brother," he slipped in, between measures.

"Nice singing," Haskell said.

"I dig your hair."

"I see Tom Jones later. I say hello for you."

The buzz from the crowd was maddening. Hypnotic faces. Screams from one corner; collapsing sighs of disappointment from another. Cards and chips spread over soft green velvet. The hum and whirl of slot machines, rolling on and on; an occasional winner dropped to his knees to collect the downpour of coins.

"Place your bets!"

"Can I get you a drink?"

"Would you like a card, sir?"

"How many more chips? Are you cashing in for the night?"

Gamblers shuffled hurriedly across the thick red carpet. White Roman columns of sculpted marble lined the entranceway to the hotel, as well as the casino.

At Caesars Palace, late into the night, Haskell was betting the combinations 14, 16, 25 feverishly, laying claim to those numbers, making them his alone.

"Sixteen. The distinguished gentleman wins again," the roulette spinner decreed.

A crowd gathered around Haskell as stacks of chips rose at his side, towering against his face. With each spin, onlookers continued to edge toward him, a desperate mob pushing forward, mistaking Haskell's fuzzy hair and boundless luck for a rabbit's foot.

"Look at the old man," said a feverish-looking bettor who hadn't been to sleep in days. "He's on fire."

"I want what he's got," said another, tie loosened, caressing a glass of Scotch.

The spectators around the table had already seen their chips disappear, their own lucky numbers—birthdays, anniversaries, addresses—now cursed digits, never to be relied on again. The bettors lingered on, however, trying to forget their own losses, perhaps looking to find another way to have a good time. Watch the other suckers get their due. But Haskell seemed to have the hot hands, the magic touch. Oddly, perhaps because of his age and his cheerful, unassuming manner, there didn't seem to be much resentment about Haskell cleaning up at the casino.

I absorbed a few shoves from behind, and then pleaded, "What do you say, Uncle? Quit while you're ahead? They're about to kick you out of here anyway. You've outworn your welcome."

"Fourteen, sixteen, twenty-five," Haskell repeated determinedly, shuffling mounds of chips over into velvet-trimmed boxes on the table. He wasn't listening to me; he was enjoying the night, the adulation from the crowd, the sudden increase in his net worth.

"Twenty-five," the roulette maestro announced. "The man with the nice hair wins again."

And yet another roar of admiration. An elegant-looking woman with frosted yellow hair and a fur wrapped over her shoulders glanced at Haskell and lifted a glass of champagne as a tribute, as a salutation, as a seduction. Haskell nodded and then smiled at me, making sure that I didn't miss the impression he was making.

Haskell played three more spins, and then cashed in his winnings, but not before taking a whirl at the wheel of chance, and landing on fourteen.

"This is a nice place," he said, tipping a cocktail waitress and lifting a cognac into his mouth.

We left the casino well into the early morning hours. The sounds of defeated junketeers, bound for home, rustled in the lobby. Worn-out zombies walked into the neon night, stumbling into traffic, toward the buses and taxis. Haskell was fine, standing a head taller—not in ego, but in cash. "It is a survivor's trick," he was telling me, "a way to hide money." He laid his winnings down flat in his shoes, and walked on them, as though wearing expensive but ill-fitting inner soles.

I shrugged coolly at the revelation, seeming not to care much anymore. My usual taste for Holocaust lore had been exhausted. It was late. I was due for a nap. We headed in the direction of the bus back to Manhattan.

As we rocked back and forth toward the city, I felt gloomy, still empty. Just before we nodded off, Haskell said, "There is a sadness in you that won't let go. You must let it go."

The next day Haskell asked if he could attend my class.

"I would like to see what you do. I have a special interest in the subject, you know."

"That's funny, I would have thought a Yankee game would have been more your pleasure today," I said mockingly.

"Ah yes, baseball—this too I would like, but not now. Come, we go to your students."

We traveled up the elevator at Hunter College. A stocky man with a beet-red face sat on a little stool, steering a lever and navigating the car from floor to floor.

"Fourteen," he announced.

"That's our floor," I said.

"And my number," Haskell reminded me.

We arrived late. Students were chatting amongst themselves. Two Hispanic girls were in the front row, chewing gum, trading whispers. A few other kids were bunched up in the center, all in jeans, baseball caps turned the wrong way. A loner sat in the back, slouched in his seat, chewing the fingernails of one hand, wearing a pair of black Dr. Martens boots laced up high along his legs, stretched out in front of him.

The final exam was in a few weeks, and with their journals already completed, there was nothing left to do but wait for my tardy arrival.

"Okay, settle down," I began. "We have a special visitor today." I looked over at Haskell, seated in the front row with his hands folded. "A guest lecturer, actually." Haskell, the Belgian hatmaker, promoted to visiting scholar in Holocaust studies at Hunter College, bypassing all those formal academic presentments. Who better to guide my students through the dark forest of remembrance than someone who had actually been there? And what better way for me to hear this canny uncle finally recite his tale? "I've decided to hand over the last class to Haskell Posner, my uncle."

We hadn't discussed the role I had in mind for him, but Haskell was neither intimidated nor troubled by subterfuge. He stood by his seat and faced my students. He then strolled tentatively over to the front of the room. I wandered off into the back, trying to vaporize from sight, giving him full reign over the class.

Before he began, he looked out into his young audience. I wondered how they might respond to him. Ordinarily so apathetic about everything—and from a generation not particularly impressed with the experience that comes with age—I feared that they might not show him the proper respect, or worse, laugh at his accent, or mock what he had to say. But the opposite proved true. As soon as he began speaking, I noticed that they seemed much more alert and genuinely interested than at any time when I had spoken to them. Perhaps they had been waiting for this Posner all along.

"I don't have a prepared lecture," he said shyly. "Unlike my nephew, I am not an educated man. Such books he has in his flat—from here to there," his open palm climbed from his knees to the top of his head. "I think he has read them all."

The class let out a nervous, supportive laugh.

"What to say? Where to begin? Who would believe?" Each question was punctuated by an exhausted Jewish sigh. "To my nephew I don't want to say such things. These stories do him no good. He likes them too much. So I tell you, and hope that my story helps your studies, not just in Adam's course, but in life.

"The Germans forced us to move from Stuttgart. 'Relocation,' they called it. We would be happy in Warsaw, they said. Ah, yes, happy," he said, sighing. "Our whole family lived in one small room in the ghetto, suffocating. All of us, uncles, aunts, nieces, nephews, the children—ah, so many children. Your teacher's father, my brother, was there."

Some students turned around in their seats, searching me out, making sure that I was paying attention.

"The conditions in the ghetto were terrible—filth everywhere, people living on the streets, families without food, no reason to live. The ghetto was small. So many all together.

"Adam's father, his name was Sam, was a young man, maybe twenty-eight. He was a fighter, a leader, an organizer. From the first day in the ghetto, he was planning to escape, to resist, to fight back. He knew. We all wanted to hope for better—the decency of the Germans, the Poles; that the Americans and the British would come. Others looked to God. Sam was meeting with other resisters. Trying to contact Poles on the other side of the wall. Bribing the ghetto police for information.

"For months Adam's father was smuggling guns into the flat. Our mother was afraid. She would say: 'The Germans will find out and kill us all. Why must you be an army by yourself?' And she was right. One day the Gestapo came. They smashed through the door. Not even a knock," he said, tapping away with a closed fist into the air; "the whole door flew into the flat. An informer told them that our family was hiding guns.

"Two officers they were. Long shiny black boots, curved hats with nice creases on the top. One of them, a heavy man with blond hair and swollen cheeks, asked, 'Where are the guns? We know they are here.' The guns were hidden. Adam's father built a cabinet underneath the wood floor. The other officer, a young man—tall, a smooth face, just shaving—was standing right on top of it."

A student gasped, shutting her eyes as though watching a late-night movie, hoping that when she chose to see again, Haskell and his story would be gone.

"No one in our family could even breathe. 'Where are the guns?' the older officer yelled again. Everyone was too afraid to speak, to move. So he said, 'Tell me where they are and who was hiding them, or I will kill you all. I will start with the oldest and then finish with the rest.'

"My mother started to cry, her lips trembling. My father grabbed hold of her, and buried his face in her hair. They didn't know what to do. They could save the family, except for Sam. But how can a parent give up a son to death? And how would they know if they could trust the Germans? The whole family could be killed, anyway. We all looked at each other, not knowing what to do.

" 'I'm waiting for your answer!' he demanded. The fire in his voice did not unfreeze our mouths, or our legs. And just then, he took out a gun from his belt and shot my father dead.

"I remember the sound of the gun. Who could forget? So loud in such a small flat.

"Father slipped from Mother's arms and fell to the floor. The officer's actions scared the younger officer. He jumped in the air; his heavy boots made a big sound when he came down, just above the trapdoor. This is where the guns were, remember?" Haskell reminded us all. "The young officer went to the older one and said, 'Our orders were to find the guns, not to kill. We don't know if the guns are here. We should search first.' 'Nonsense,' said the other, and then, without moving his legs, he turned his face and shot our mother.

" 'Where are the guns?' he repeated.

"This was too much. One sister fainted immediately. A brother dropped to his knees and cried like a baby. He was now an orphan. The two Gestapo officers began to argue. The younger one threatened the older, saying he would report him. He called him a murderer. The older officer didn't mind this; he wasn't finished with the family. But first, while the younger officer was still shouting, waving his arms in the air, the older man shot him in the stomach and killed him. The older officer started to laugh. 'Fool, what business do you have to protect Jews?'

"The Gestapo officer would have killed us all—one by one. But while the two Germans were arguing, Sam found a gun. I don't even know where from—so many places he was hiding them," Haskell said, chuckling, "and shot the Gestapo officer six times. Six times! He walked toward the man, shooting with each step. By the last two shots, he was standing above him. He then threw the gun down at the murderer's face and ran out of the flat. I never saw my brother again until after the war. Somehow he escaped from the ghetto and joined the partisans. The rest of the family was taken to Auschwitz. All my other brothers and sisters, most of the children, were gassed there."

The two girls in the front row were crying. Some faces had a mesmerized look. Those in the middle and back of the classroom were speechless.

Haskell wiped his face, and continued, "Ah, what else to say? My story is finished, yes."

No one said a word. No applause. No questions. Perhaps the students were looking for me to break the silence. But I hadn't heard this story before, either. It was my first time as well. I wasn't prepared to take over. There was more to the mystery of my silent father than I had dared realize.

A week later Haskell had taken ill. There was a message on my answering machine from a doctor at Columbia Presbyterian. "Mr. Posner, your uncle has suffered a heart attack. You should come quickly."

I took a taxi and got out at 165th and Broadway. Through the revolving doors, up the elevator, and then, sliding across sanitized tiles, through the stark corridors, I arrived at the cardiac care unit. I nodded at the attendant as I whizzed by her station.

"Excuse me, sir," she said, an arm raised in the air, "you'll have to check in."

"No time for that, sorry," I replied, quickly peeking inside each partition. Old men, breathing slowly, recuperating—all so desperate for the miracle of an extended warranty.

Blinking gadgets resonated heartbeats in many directions. Hard to separate the machines from the men. My own chest tightened amidst this ticking chorus.

"Where is he?" I asked, glimpsing through yet another divider. "Pardon me."

Still no sign of Haskell. Perhaps he had already been cured, shuttled out of intensive care to make room for patients who were really sick—those insufficiently tested as survivors. How could his heart possibly fail him? Haskell had endured so much; surely he could withstand the excitement of New York, and the reunion with his nephew. A momentary lightness passed over me. I thought to warn the nurses on the floor—particularly the more attractive ones—that my uncle would soon be paying them a visit.

I neared the last curtain on the row. There was Haskell. A flat line registered on the monitor. He had already died, alone.

Haskell journeyed by himself, at his age, to breathe new life into his nephew. Now he was all tapped out, neglecting to leave something over for himself.

An oxygen tent hovered around his bed like a transparent shield. His nose was stuffed with tubes; needles, strategically placed to sustain life, clung to his veins.

He was completely bald, the helmet gone. There was to be no camouflage here. Death could not be fooled.

His arms were laid flat with open palms. Even through the hazy tent I could make out the blue numbers: 14, 16, 25—the winning combinations, easy to remember, permanently branded on his arm.

ELIJAH
VISIBLE

"That's it! I've had enough," Adam announced as he rose from his chair, gesturing wildly. A piece of matzo crunched in his fist. "Look at us! Just look at us. This is pathetic. You call *this* a Seder?"

A short woman with dark hair and a screechy voice was seated at the head of the table. "What's wrong?" Sylvia replied, looking up. She had been mumbling away in some phonetic adherence to Hebrew scripture, her eyes moving in the altogether wrong direction—left to right in doctored English. To all those in the room, it was a seance of incomprehensible words, the mother tongue of orphans in the Diaspora, pig Latin for nonkosher Jews. "We're following all the rules, sort of. . . ."

"Rules? What rules?" Adam insisted. "Since when do you play Elvis Costello at a Seder? Where is that written? Show me in the Haggadah!"

"Shush," Miriam said, "he's singing, 'Everyday I Write the Book.' You know that's my favorite Elvis Costello song."

"Yeah, I know, but that's not the book I'm talking about," Adam said, and then sighed, defeatedly.

A far cry from the family's origins in Poland. Rabbinic grandfathers, observant fathers—now a new generation of fragmented legacies, American torchbearers skilled in the art of cultural compromise.

"It's just background music," Miriam said. "It keeps the whole thing moving at a nice, brisk pace. We need something to cut down on the boredom."

Miriam was Sylvia's older sister, and Adam, their younger cousin. Through a powerful mixture of grit, fortitude, and old-fashioned *mazel,* the Posner family had survived the Holocaust, and now this—the bickering of unrepentant legacies—was all that remained.

Miriam was seated by herself at the side pocket of the table. Unmarried, middle-aged, and miserable, a victim of life's elusive pageantry. She sat there, slumped over, her blond hair swaying above a bowl of golden chicken soup. Steamy vapors rose up against her face, leaving a radiance on her cheeks that would be gone by dessert. With each shake or turn of her head, gilded costume earrings danced wildly in the air.

"You know how they play music at an aerobics class?" she asked.

"Yes," Adam replied, sensing an improbable analogy in the making.

" 'Move to the beat, ladies: up and down, left and right, twist from side to side, right elbow to the left leg, flex those stomach muscles, tighten those behinds!' Well, anyway, that's how they do it at the New York Health and Racquet Club."

"So? What kind of Seder do they have? It already sounds more formal than this."

"No! You're missing the point. You see, the music makes it all easier, it makes all the difference in the world. I couldn't do a sit-up without it. And now that's what we're doing here: davening to the beat." Her hands slashed through the air lithely, measuring notes and meters, as she sang: 'Bless the matzo, one, two, three . . . one, two, three; point to the celery, five, six, seven, eight; make a horseradish sandwich, all together now—*dayenu.'* " She stopped suddenly, and listened to catch her cadence. No doubt confused by the twisting melodies—the British punk, the mocking Hebrew—that competed for reverence. "Get it? Now lighten up and eat your soup."

All in all, this was a typical Posner family Seder. A yearly Sheepshead Bay ritual, held in Sylvia's home off Ocean Avenue. For the past ten years, ever since all the parents of these cousins had died, the Seder, which had once been a solemn and sanctified event, was reduced to a carnival. The informality was seductive, rampant—and everywhere. White yarmulkes lay folded on the table like crescent half-moons—untouched, unworn. The occasional mistake—the lighting of the menorah—inspired no alarm, no tremor of religious infraction. There was a barren Seder plate shimmering in the glow of a hanging chandelier. The reflected light caused an unnatural blinding, which served the assembled moods quite well. The four questions went unasked, as though the Posner family didn't want to know the answers, and were sapped of all curiosity. A stack of matzo lay idly by amidst slices of yeast-infested pumpernickel.

Sylvia's two Akitas bounded around excitedly, followed by her children, their tails and limbs almost indistinguishable. The madness and mayhem of their circuit wasn't at all related to the strategic concealing of the *afikomen*—that middle piece of matzo hidden somewhere in the home, with a present to its finder. For that Adam might not have minded the commotion. But these diversions were not ceremonial in nature. The children were chasing one another, but not in reenactment of the Exodus. The ancient contest between the Egyptians and the Jews seemed of only modest interest, lacking as it did the cyberdrama of the Mighty Morphin Power Rangers and the Teenage Mutant Ninja Turtles.

"I won't eat my soup," Adam insisted. "This is all a sacrilege. A disgrace, a *shande*. Am I the only person in this room with a conscience?"

The sisters had been snapping their fingers at the table, not in recitation of plagues but in lyrical appreciation of some other punk riff.

"Is anybody listening?"

Sylvia's husband, Angelo, was attuned to Adam's laments, but he didn't dare speak, nor was he likely to interfere. Angelo was a Bensonhurst native, a graduate of St. Anthony's Academy for Boys. He had been schooled by nuns and had spent more than a year of afternoons hanging out at the local corner with his friends, most of whom dreamed of becoming either a prize-fighter or a gangster. Angelo had taken an entirely different career path. He became a Jew by conscription, talked into it at the insistence of Sylvia's parents, and the indifference of his own.

Upon his admission into the tribe, Angelo took his place in the family's furrier business on West Twenty-seventh Street. While friends from the old neighborhood continued to shoot craps and run numbers, he became a stable family man and a fixture of Seventh Avenue.

Angelo's ascent came with a price. He was no longer a tough guy—not in the neighborhood, not even in his own home. When Bernard Posner, Sylvia and Miriam's father, was alive, Angelo took orders from him and suffered his indignities.

"I need more spools of leather!" Bernard would yell out in the factory. "Who was in charge of the order? Where is that dumb goy, my son-in-law?" he would joke. But was it a joke? In time, all those at the factory, including Angelo, understood that "goy" was not meant as an endearment—even when reserved for a son-in-law.

Once Bernard died, it became Sylvia's turn to run the business—and Angelo.

"Where is my guinea husband?"

It was as though Angelo's spine had collapsed; the accelerated decay proved to be of no concern to anyone.

The journey from Catholic to Jew for Angelo Andrini took him as far as the ritual bath and the unsparing circumcision; after that, he was mute in matters regarding Jewish observances. He awkwardly declined all offers to lead the Seder, forever humbled by the obligation to carry on the patriarchal duties of a religion only recently known to him.

Straining to hear Adam, Sylvia said, "How about some gefilte fish to calm your nerves?"

"This isn't about gefilte fish!" Adam insisted.

"Well, what then?" Sylvia asked.

"It's all this mockery. We've made the Seder meaningless. We're not really Jews."

"We're not?" Angelo inquired, a bit perplexed and troubled. Left behind in Bensonhurst was not only his Catholicism, but also a small memento of his manhood. Switching teams hadn't been easy. You don't simply trade in one uniform for another. The Italian gangs of his youth had their tribal initiations; Jewish rabbis had theirs. In recognition of his religious transformation, Angelo was left with a genital battle scar—the removal of precious foreskin. Not a pleasant procedure for an adult, even if it meant, in this case, the promise of a better life, and receiving the acceptance of Sylvia's parents.

But now, after all that, Adam had announced that no one at the table was Jewish—not even the one person who had shed blood for the privilege of being a Posner. All these years Angelo assumed that he had negotiated a more durable membership.

"Don't listen to him, dear," Sylvia interrupted. "We're all Jews, and so are you."

Adam cast his arms across the table as though he were about to audition for the role of Moses. "What's this for?" he said, pointing angrily toward a stack of magazines on the table. Besides the horseradish and the bitter herbs were back issues of *Glamour* and *Elle*. "Are the two of you hoping to get dolled up for Elijah's visit? What's the latest fashion for a Hebrew slave girl, nowadays?"

"Are you through yet?" Miriam asked.

"We should all go back to Egypt and beg the Pharaoh's forgiveness. We should have never left in the first place if this is where we were headed. We were better off as slaves. It's time to repent our sins."

Finally, a way for Angelo to contribute with prayer. Recalling memories of St. Anthony's, he said, "I can teach you all about that, Adam. I still remember confession. I converted, but when the rabbi told me I was Jewish, I kept my fingers crossed behind my back.

You know, I didn't want Our Savior to be mad at me. So, anyway, if you're looking to repent, a few Hail Marys is what you gotta do. And maybe . . ."

"Shut up, Angelo!" Sylvia snapped. She then reminded her cousin, "You know, I was in Egypt two years ago. I got news for you: they have *Glamour* there, too, and Elvis Costello. You'd still be in bondage."

"I find this way of celebrating Passover somehow worse," Adam said.

"What's gotten into you, anyway?" Sylvia shot back. "We do the Seder like this every year. You never said anything before."

"I always wanted to."

"Oh, give me a break. When all of a sudden did you become so religious?" Miriam added.

Stroking her chin as her father once did at the head of the table, Sylvia announced, "This isn't about the Seder at all. Admit it. It's the letter, that goddamned letter!"

Adam's facial response suggested that Sylvia was right; something was burning inside him, which had nothing to do with the foliage on Mount Sinai. Adam had not intended to sabotage the Seder. Each year the ritual had become more corrupted, but he still kept coming back. There had been no exodus from Sheepshead Bay so far; although quite a few times he had considered not showing up, he ultimately decided to stay with his tribe. But this year would be different, and his rebellion, long-suppressed, would make the Seder's demise inevitable.

Sylvia was right—this wasn't about the Seder. A week earlier, in the mail from Belgium, had come a letter from cousin Artur, the jeweler from Antwerp.

As much as the Posner children regarded themselves as the end of the line, the final chapter in the family's unredeemed saga, that wasn't at all true. There was Artur in Belgium and Chaim in Israel. Cousins also. Partners in legacy. Men now in their early seventies. Elders with seniority, in genealogical rank, and in suffering. Artur had survived the camps, Chaim had escaped Hitler by emigrating to Palestine.

But Adam and his cousins had been raised to ignore the lineage that was unalterably theirs. There was a calculated silence in all things associated with the past. And for good reason. The Posners were related not just in blood, but also in experience, in memory. There was a conscious avoidance of bringing together those who knew, who had been there, with those of the next generation, who were witnesses to nothing but the silences, and the screams. Such bonding could only be undertaken sparingly. To look in one another's eye was to acknowledge what had been done, and lost; a flashing mirror of missing faces; a stunning recollection of the horror with all too painful accuracy—a group photograph of a large family with ghosts standing in for those no longer of this world.

At the same time, and pathetically more curious, was not the profound silence, but the rifts among themselves. The parents— the American brothers—were often at war with one another. The nephews, without regard to continent, hardly spoke. Cousins didn't acknowledge one another's existence. It would have taken all the resources of the United Nations to mediate these varied and senseless disputes, and still no assurance of a cease-fire.

The treachery of the Holocaust was only a nasty prologue in their family's destruction. The rest was performed with their own hands, by their own neglect.

Who knows how the ancient anger began? This uncle said that about this nephew; a letter failed to get answered; each generation gave the other the finger. Separated by thousands of miles of ocean, the insult managed to land in Brooklyn, without the aid of air traffic controllers or visible landing strips.

The parents had only wanted better for their children; what they gave them instead was the impulse for dissension and shame.

Artur's letter was brief, and to the point:

16/3/94

Dearest Cousins,

Please forgive my English. It is not so good.

I write you now because I am getting old. When I was a young man, after the camps, when I had time to think about what happened, I realized that I was already old. I had lost my childhood. I lost my early manhood. I lost most of my family. I lived a whole life in a short time. That's what happens in a time of madness. It is hard to believe I am still here.

I know I have little time left in this world. Perhaps the next one will be kinder to me.

Most of our family was murdered during the war. All who survived, like your parents, had murdered minds. I know your parents did not speak much about Europe. For them it was a graveyard, no more a place of memories. They wanted to forget. They deceived themselves. It was not so easy for me, either.

I am sending you a list of uncles, aunts, and cousins who you never met, who you will never know. You and your children carry the seeds of their memories. It is a great responsibility for you, but you must live a life that gives meaning to their death, and comfort to their souls.

We are all that is left of the Posner family. Before I die, I would like to know my cousins better. Your fathers and I were arguing for years. Fights over money. Over inheritance. After all we suffered, the family was still divided. We, who suffered so much from real enemies, now fighting with each other. Such nonsense. I hope this is not how you live together.

I watch American television here in Antwerp. I hear this American phrase, "bury the hatchet." This too we should do. Before it is too late for me; before it is too late for you.

I come for a visit. To see you. To know you. To tell you, in person, our family history. Your children should know what happened. They must continue to remind the world.

We must learn the lessons from the fire.

Warmest regards,
Artur

"Yes, it is the letter," Adam acknowledged.

"What's the big deal?" Sylvia said, mechanically cutting into the breast of a roast chicken. "So we got a letter from the old man in Belgium."

"He's not just an old man, he's our cousin."

"Cousin, my ass. The bottom line is that he's trying to sponge a trip to America off of us, and who knows what else he needs."

"That's how you read the letter?"

"Yes. I already wrote him back."

"You did?"

"Yes, that's right, I did. I told him that we're not interested, that we're too busy. The kids are in school, we're swamped at the factory. Tell him, Angelo."

"She's right," Angelo said obligingly.

"He's not coming to see us because of that bullshit. You don't think he'll realize how lame those excuses are? He'll know you just don't want to see him."

"So, what do I care if he figures it out? And why would you care? You've never met the man. And I don't recall you stopping our fathers when they trashed him. And frankly, if I remember right, you had some of the funnier lines about him when you were a kid. 'Artur, the twerp from Antwerp,'" she said in a mock accent. "That was you."

"Fine, I've grown up. That's what happens with age."

"Well leave us out of it, then," Sylvia said.

"I can't believe you weren't moved by that letter. How could you ignore the man's pain, his past, everything he's been through?

You've missed the whole point. He's trying to save *us*, save us all."

"Save us?" Miriam asked. "Save us from what? We're perfectly fine. He should save himself."

"Yeah, and all that stuff about 'burying the hatchet,' " Angelo observed. "What does he know? We're better than him, right?"

"The man is a fraud," Sylvia added.

"Daddy said that he took money from him," Miriam said.

Adam became enraged. "What are you talking about? Are we starting again with this childishness? I thought we could have buried all this with our parents. But instead, we're carrying it on. . . ."

"It's true," Miriam reiterated. "Daddy never forgave Artur for borrowing money and never paying it back."

"This is what it all comes down to? A cousin writes you a letter. He's at the end of his life. He's a Holocaust survivor. He wants to restore some honor to this family, and all you two can see is some cynical attempt to extort money from you?"

"Exactly," Sylvia said. "If my father couldn't forgive him, then neither can we. We're a family, and we have to stick together, right Angelo?"

"Artur's our family too, but who's sticking up for him?"

"I guess it's you," Angelo said.

"Who said your father was right? He wasn't exactly the most sensible person. How do you know that Artur ever borrowed money from Bernard? How can you be so sure that he never paid it back?"

"Because he didn't, that's why," Miriam said, instinctively.

"This is insane. I can't believe I'm even having this conversation."

"Good, then let's stop and finish the Seder," Miriam said. "And Sylvia, could you put on a new CD?"

Sylvia ignored her sister's wishes; the disc player remained empty and silent, while slowly the room became filled with renewed discord. "You know, you're just like your father," Sylvia said. "You don't know the value of a dollar."

"What is that supposed to mean?"

"Money means nothing to you, you, such a high-minded

teacher; and that father of yours, a writer, is that what they call it? Your father never made a success of himself in America, so it was easy for him—and now you—to think nothing of someone stealing money."

"Wait a minute, who said Artur stole money?"

"What he did was the same as stealing," Sylvia said, "right, Angelo?"

"Yeah."

"You can't see past the money, past your father's petty little dramas. There's this incredible letter that should be placed in the Holocaust Museum, it should be encased in Yad Vashem, and you're talking about a few hundred dollars' loan."

"Oh no, it was at least a thousand," Miriam added. "Not to mention a few collect phone calls he made to our father."

"That's right," Sylvia said, "I forgot about those collect calls. Way to go, Mir."

"Is everybody bananas here?" Adam wanted to know.

Just then there came the sound of a crash from an adjoining room. The runaway train of children—the mischievous offspring of former slaves—had caused an accident of some sort.

"Jason! What's going on in there?" Sylvia shrieked, and then dispatched Angelo to find out what had occurred. Within seconds, and out of habit from his bumblings at the factory, she followed after him.

In a whisper, Miriam turned to Adam and said, "You know our father paid for your bar mitzvah."

"So?"

"So you could show a little more loyalty to him as we continue his battles, that's all."

"What battles? You're fighting a Holocaust survivor who lives on the other side of the Atlantic? You already outnumber him on your own. This is all so sadistic, like you're trying to finish the job that the Nazis started."

Before she had time to reply, Adam got up and announced, "I've had enough. I'm getting out of here."

As Adam headed for the door, Sylvia returned, took a sweeping turn toward her cousin, and said, "You're just jealous that my father made something of himself in this country."

Adam slowly edged back toward the table. "Jealous? Jealous of what? Your father was a moron, a semi-illiterate. You've forgotten that he used to struggle through the comics. That was the big achievement of his day. We'd all have to recite the *Shema* if he could make it all the way to "Dear Abby." The man was petty— and mean. Always putting people down, holding grudges, isolating members of his own family. I see the two of you have done a great job carrying on in his absence." Checking to see whether Angelo was still in the other room, Adam continued. "Remember the way he used to treat Angelo, like some dog off the street? This is the man whose judgment I should trust, whose fights I should honor?"

"Fine, don't respect Daddy's wishes," Sylvia said. "But we're his children, and this is Passover. We're commanded to honor our mother and father."

"That's about the most tortured reading of the Ten Commandments I've ever heard."

"Well, if you don't understand, then you can just go ahead and leave."

Adam realized then that they had all become strangers. They were cousins who claimed an essential closeness, but they didn't really know one another. Like any family, their union was completely involuntary. The configuration of relationships, of animosities, of resentments and loyalties, was assembled without asking anyone's opinion, or preference. Only Angelo had made a conscious decision to join, and then found himself forever a prisoner of his own identity—the lapsed Catholic, the unrealized thug.

"Maybe it's not about the money at all. Have you considered that?" Adam suggested. "Maybe it's about something else."

"Like what?" Miriam asked.

"Like maybe you're afraid to know the past, to know the truth. It's hard enough just being a Jew on the IRT, heading into the city for work. Why would anyone want to know the whole tortured history? The baggage is heavy enough as it is. So you pamper yourself—information enters only on a need-to-know basis. Listen to the music we play around here; we've lost our soul. We don't know who we are, where we come from, why we should care about tomorrow. Your kids are running around here like a couple of zombies; it could be Easter for all they know."

Angelo had returned. "It *is* Easter," he reminded all, boastfully, "same time, this year."

"Quiet, Angelo!" Sylvia blurted. "Like what truths?"

"Like how they were all in the camps, how my father saved your father's life. Your father had given up hope, but my father pushed him to go on. They stole bread from other prisoners. They cheated. There were always fights in the camp. My father once had to kill someone in order to survive. Imagine all the shame, the guilt. And they couldn't do anything about all those other relatives who died, who they weren't able to save."

Suddenly, a rush of forbidden screams, tired silences, and soft whimpers flooded the Seder. It began to sink in, although only imperceptibly so.

"There's more. Artur had a rougher time than they did. He was a child in Auschwitz. His parents killed. An orphan, marked for selection three different times. That's the man you don't want to have visit you; the man who wants your spoiled, healthy children to know him, to remember him."

Sylvia's face remained impassive, her expression resolute. She was not about to surrender her emotions to Adam's calculated melodrama.

"Did you know your father was married before the war?" Adam continued. "This was long before he met your mother. You want to know what happened to her?"

"I don't want to hear this!" Miriam screamed.

"You should know. She was murdered while being taken to the camps. Hit in the stomach with a rifle butt. She was six months' pregnant."

Gently, slowly, very unsure of himself, Adam walked over to the couch and reached into the pocket of his jacket. Out came a black-and-white photo, which, delicately, he took over to his cousins. It was a picture of a frightened-looking woman in a simple white dress. "This is her—your father's first wife. I found it stored away in a closet—inside a box that I swore I would never get to."

"Why now?" Sylvia asked.

"Why not?"

There was a momentary silence. Even the roughhousing children and yapping dogs seemed to observe the moment, quiet at last in another room.

"It's all in the family history that Artur sent. Read it. It's hard to take. A bitter pill. You can only read short passages at a time. Our parents concealed everything from us. Too much guilt, I guess. Too much regret. We can't afford to do that again. We owe it to the children, to ourselves—there's too much at stake."

That night the universe was filled with Jews celebrating Passover. And in every home, an invisible ghost, a former prophet, appeared and sipped a mere taste of wine. Elijah the Prophet, dressed in beggar's clothes, the harbinger of messianic deliverance, resolver of all disputes—with so much to do, and so much to drink.

The door opens in the spirit of an invitation. Children hover above the brim of a specially designated cup, hoping to see whether Elijah had come to the well this year. This is the tradition. Some believe and say the accompanying prayers, others just leave the wine and open the door. There was once the faith that Elijah would appear and grace the home, in much the same way as ancient ancestors, confronted with an altogether different ghost, waited in terror for the angel of death to pass over theirs.

But in Sylvia Posner Andrini's home, a full cup of wine remained on the table. No one bothered to measure. Elijah never came. Much revealed itself that night—ghostly encounters, voices from the dead, unearthed feelings—but nothing suitable for the holiday. The cup remained heavy, like the assembled hearts of the Posner family.

The next day, across the Atlantic, Artur, with his own money, bought a round-trip ticket—as he had always planned—to America. Elijah had not visited the Posners that year, but Cousin Artur was on his way.

BINGO
BY THE
BUNGALOW

The woman was eccentric, even for the Catskills. Actually, she was crazy, but that's not the kind of silent confession a child can easily allow about his mother. It takes a measure of distance to appreciate the abnormality. Blind faith in parental credentials is a virtue of childhood, but one day it vanishes. The brittle truce that lies between the gap in generations gives way to new realities, and empathies.

But then the entire colony was filled with crazies. It was a summer loony bin of refugees from the fallen Europe, now resettled in America, spending the months of June through August in Sullivan County—"the country" as they called it. Cohen's Summer Cottages was made up of ten white-boarded bungalows scattered across a lush green field. Small boxy frames with ash roof tiles. Each cottage had a porch and swinging door that clapped firmly against the frame. A stone walkway linking the cottages—a trail for the dispossessed. A lone, rickety shed—home for a lawn mower and washing machine—rested beneath an ancient weeping willow. There was a taut clothesline that stretched from the swings to the slide. On windy afternoons, a United Nations of underwear and brassieres would flap restlessly in the breeze.

"It's over eighty-five degrees today," Hyman Cohen announced, returning from the shed, the first of many daily readings of the mercury stick. "*Ach,* imagine that, eighty-five, like an oven . . . but dry," he said, shaking his head in disbelief, and spitting to the side.

The thermometer always gave the same reading, and he the same response.

Cohen wore an oversized pair of orange cabana shorts with silver crests that trimmed the waistband. His skin was dark and rough; his hair and eyebrows thick and unruly. One of his legs appeared lifeless. He dragged it about as if chained to some burden no one could see.

It was his colony, a piece of real land, paid for in cash to mask the memories from five years before. His tenants shared in his addiction: the need to escape and forget—the smoke, the shaved heads, the ancestral remains. Each a survivor from one camp or another: Bergen-Belsen, Maidanek, Treblinka, Auschwitz. Left behind was a sacred burial ground. The geographic sacrifice. No time, or courage, to place a wreath or a tombstone. Simply too hard to go back.

The music of the colony resonated with the sounds of atonal displacement. Everyone spoke with some mangled, confused accent that had been forced on them in America. English learned in a hurry. Verbs and nouns swallowed without time to digest. Some vowels never made it into the vocabulary, abandoned heedlessly at the docks.

Where better should this horde of runaways, of phantoms, have settled in for the summer? Cohen's was strangely their home. They were safe here—well, as safe as they would ever allow themselves to feel. There was much they could never believe in again. Faith was lost. No god. No humanity. No good places to hide. Cohen's at least offered a refuge of shared cynicism.

And in doing so, it also tolerated a fair amount of dementia. All that insanity added to the atmospheric diversity of the place, like the cool mountain night air and the morning dew. The refugees could swim in Kiamisha Lake. Do as the ancient Indians: purge the sins, cleanse the soul, dive deep into the belly of the water— where it's quiet—hoping to silence the stowaway shrieks that had come along for the ride.

Cohen never liked the word *concentration camp,* preferring instead the German *lager.*

"Why a camp, they should call it? Belsen was no camp, no picnic. In America, camp is where you send the children, or where

you learn to be a Communist. We shouldn't call the *lager* a camp."
And then, prideful of the haven he offered, he would add: "You
want to know from a camp? This is a camp . . . right here. My camp!
An American camp, not for children, but for the people like us. We
don't march. We play cards all day. We sing, we cry. We look out
at the trees. No fences, no wires. . . . Now, who wants for pinochle?"

Written on the swinging sign at the foot of the stone road,
carved into the wood in seductive script, read:

COHEN'S SUMMER COTTAGES
LEISURE *MACHT FREI*

"Keep up with me, you're falling behind," Rosa said. She was wearing a black polka-dot dress with flowing chiffon lace that floated
in the air. Moving smartly between branches and twigs, she cut
through the woods like an animal beginning its evening hunt.

"I can't walk this fast," a whining voice trailed her brisk pace,
"it's too dark. . . . I'm tripping over acorns."

The sky was seared in blackness. A few resilient stars wriggled
free of the buried pack. With flashlights, mother and son made
their way into the forest. Beams sliced between trees, startling mos-
quitoes, overexposing fireflies, scattering milky streaks through
the bushes.

"We're going to be late for my game," she said. "Do you want
your mama to miss her bingo game? Think what we could win."

From behind and stammering: "What can we win?"

"Let's see . . ." she ruminated, pointing the flashlight down
against her side, a white mist of light dappling the ground. "They
have a blender and a seltzer maker. Ida, next door, tells me there
is a bagel slicer; you just put the bagel in a plastic cover, and then
slice like regular. No more cutting my hand. Such good prizes, no?"

"We'll never use any of that junk—even if we do win." The
child was not easily tempted by convenience, nor fooled by deceit.

"Don't argue with me," she said. "I need to practice for the big game when summer is over—the one at Cohen's. He offers a cash grand prize."

"Why do we have to go? Can't we just stay home tonight? Lucy's on television."

Rosa turned around, lifted the flashlight, and planted a perfect moon over her face. In a possessed voice she said, "What do you think puts food on our table?"

"Bingo?"

"Bingo!"

"How does a bagel slicer put food on our table?"

"Every little bit helps."

"But we went last night. . . ."

"And we go tonight. Tomorrow we will go to Krause's Colony for a movie at their concession. The Three Stooges are playing. We'll have bagels, lox, and cream cheese. That you'll like."

And with that offer she danced through the woods, waving her arms like a sorceress, skipping around each tree; then she turned swiftly to flash a ray of light on her young son, who by now had resigned himself to the night's bingo game.

Two years earlier Rosa's husband had died, suddenly. His heart stopped. Just gave up. They had been two survivors who left much behind in that European graveyard—except death, which must have been lonely, or simply wasn't yet finished with the family. With Morris's parting, the task of raising Adam fell to her, alone.

Rosa Posner, fragile, a thin face with full lips, an unforgetting purple scar molded on her forehead, feared being a widow with child in a new land. Like the other refugees, she stumbled over the language. She did not know the secret handshakes that seemed so natural for immigrants who came before the war. And of course there was the concern over money. *"Ach, geld. Ich brauch mehr geld."* Her money worries never allowed her mind a minute's rest.

"I know from nothing except how to survive," she pondered. In the camps she had been a saboteur, a black-market organizer, an underground operator. It took years to relearn the simple etiquette of life among the living. "Who in this country needs to know from such things?"

They lived in a middle-class section of Brooklyn. Ethnics at every corner. Dark walk-up apartment houses. Trees planted at the foot of the curb, in front of some buildings, but not others. It was a borough built mostly of stone and concrete, not entirely in harmony with nature.

One day, joining a card game in Brooklyn, Rosa learned that she had a knack for recalling numbers, and a certain streakiness with luck that seemed to will the royalty of the deck in her direction.

She became a gambler, a regular shark at the neighborhood tables. During the day she worked in a stationery store off Nostrand Avenue—calendars, magazines, fancy pens, newspapers, especially the *Forward.* She knew them all. But at night, off to a neighborhood game for gin rummy or seven-card poker.

For three weeks each year, during the Christmas season running through the first part of January—the peak time for snowbirds—she would take Adam out of school, board a Greyhound bus, and head down to Florida. It was a long bus ride—almost two days. Adam would sleep for most of the time, or stare down at the pages of a book, or color in a large white pad that Rosa had picked up for him at the stationery store. He never complained about the trip. It was all part of his mother's therapy—he knew it, even then.

Rosa passed the time by staring out the window. She loved the long journey south, chasing the warm weather, anticipating the tropics, breezing through all those unfamiliar towns. "What is this Fayetteville, and Jacksonville? Where are we now?" The motion of the bus rocked her gently, but her eyes never closed as she struggled with all those solicitations posted along the highway. Her lips moved slowly, and then the billboard was gone, already well behind her.

But when the bus reached Miami, Rosa stepped on the warm

asphalt on Flagler Street and was immediately reminded of why she had come. There was the dog track on First Street on Miami Beach. And jai alai in Miami. The hotels along Collins Avenue were filled with "pigeons," as she called them—a phrase picked up from late-night movies, the source of much of her English.

"Now you stay in this room until I get back," she said, her son lying in bed in his pajamas, shadows from the black-and-white TV flickering off the window. Jackie Gleason droned in the background. "If you need anything, I'll be at the Caribbean Hotel, down the street. I'll come back with lots of money tonight. We'll be rich like Rockefellers. Tomorrow, I'll buy you a stuffed alligator in the souvenir store downstairs, maybe even a painted coconut. Now go to sleep."

In the country, during the summer, the games were fewer, and the stakes lower. But there was bingo, the calling of the numbers—B23, A14, G9—which serenaded her through each night.

At the top of a road littered with pinecones the forest came to a halt. There was a light that led down to a barn, a long trailerlike edifice where the whole colony gathered for bingo. Once inside, Rosa purchased eight cards.

"You play so many cards, Mrs. Posner," the man at the concession observed. "How do you keep up with all of them?"

"I brought my little helper," she replied.

The room was filled mostly with people from the colony, but there were a few, like Rosa and Adam, who traveled from neighboring villages, playing bingo wherever it could be found. Each colony offered a game a week. For some, that was more than enough.

"You'll play these two, Adam, and I'll play the rest."

They took their seats at a long wooden table with an adjoining bench, and set the cards out in front of them.

"Oh, I like these," Rosa said, uncorking a Magic Marker that had a round sponge for a head. "You see, you just push the marker down on the card like this. Watch me, you don't want to mark the wrong number."

A giant cage filled with wooden balls readied itself for the caller's rumbling spin.

"Our first prize is the bagel slicer," the caller said. "To win you got to have an L in any direction." He let go of the crank. The balls came to a crackling halt. He then opened the cage and released the first of the night's numbers.

"B seven!"

"We got one," Adam said, patting the card with his marker, his small face alternately glowing and serious. "We live in bungalow seven—that's why they called it."

Rosa smiled down at her son but remained earnest in her own vigil. As the numbers dropped from the cage, Rosa was busy blotting her card, checking up and down the rows, hands moving methodically like a spirited conductor.

Several games passed and Rosa gathered her fortune: the bagel slicer, the blender, a summer umbrella, a walking cane, a straw hat, two ashtrays—one made into the shape of a flamingo, the other a fish.

Someone in the front row screamed "Fix!" which drew a wave a laughter from the good-natured folk.

"Who is that lady back there?"

"Check her cards! Read me back her numbers again, will yah?"

"Go back to your own bungalow colony, lady!"

Rosa smiled shyly, but paid little mind to their teasings. With each call of the numbers, her eyes—fixed and hypnotic—would light up like the brightest of moons. Adam concentrated on the pageantry of his mother's luck, the lettering on her forearm raced by him, the branded marks blurred in streaks before his eyes.

His attention faltered. A disapproving Rosa leaned over and blotted in a few of the numbers that her son had missed. "Adam, you are not watching. I cannot depend on you." He, meanwhile, checked his cards once more, trying to see if the hand dealt his mother—the one on her forearm—in any way equaled a winning card. Chasing her movements, he grew sleepy. All that kept him awake was the sound of his mother's calming refrain, the lullaby of his summers:

"Bingo!"

"Bingo!"

"Bingo!"

As the night wore on, Adam dropped off to sleep, stretched out over the bench, beside Rosa. A half-eaten hamburger remained at the table. His cards failed him. So did his stamina. "Bingo!" unaccountably soothed his slumber.

Years earlier, just a few months before Morris's death, a five iron glistened in the sun. Artie was lofting golf balls out into the open blue sky. A scuff of grass, burnished on the blade, mixed with the first moisture of the day. The flight of the ball came into view against the tall green trees that surrounded the colony. On the other side of the forest were other crazies, with their own accents.

"Fore!" he yelled.

The refugees didn't have a whole lot of experience with golf in Poland and Russia, so it took a number of summers for them to realize that the avalanche of dimpled white balls—preceded by the number "four"—was not an air raid, just conspicuous recreation.

The other half of the field was occupied by Abe. He was wearing a pair of white tennis shorts and a white undershirt. At first glance, the features of his face seemed to be getting away from him. He had a fleshy nose, prominent ears, and heavy eyelids.

Abe was holding fast to a spool of cord. A kite flew above him, scattering in the wind, looping in the airy currents.

"Get that kite out of here!" Artie yelled. "I'll punch a hole right through it! Fore!"

The launching of a retaliatory golf ball did not deter Abe.

"How much of the field do you need for that stupid game?" he asked.

Artie paused and contemplated just how valuable breathing

room was to everyone at Cohen's Summer Cottages. Once imprisoned, they all now longed for space. Before coming to any conclusions on the matter, Adam, wearing blue short pants with matching suspenders and a striped blue polo shirt, circled up to him. He was pedaling a bright red fire engine, and pulling on a string that sounded a bell.

"Hey kid, come here," Artie said, his tanned face taking on a soft and tender glow.

Adam wore a red helmet that was much too large for his head. It tipped over his face like a catcher's mask.

"How's your dad?"

"He's on the porch," he replied, removing the helmet.

Artie strained his eyes and caught sight of Morris sitting on the porch of the bungalow. Artie liked Morris, considered him a real scholar, a refined and decent man, but emotionally tortured— worse even than the rest. Adam's father had survived two camps, fought in the forest as a partisan, almost died of typhus. And now a heart condition, the poor guy. Artie reached for another club— a wood this time, to satisfy his anger—and before sending the ball into fuming orbit, wondered why a man like Morris, who had suffered so much senseless pain, should not be allowed some kind of immunity from ordinary diseases, at least for a while.

"Is he feeling better?"

"Don't know," Adam said. "He can't come down from the porch."

"What do you mean?"

"Doctor said he's got to stay on the porch, or inside the bungalow. Too many steps to go up and down."

"I see. . . . Tell him I'll come by and see him later."

"Okay," and with motoring feet, the red fire engine sped away down the walking path.

Adam was the only child at Cohen's Summer Cottages. One generation removed from the awful legacy, he was their uncorrupted hope, the promise of a life unburdened by nightmare and guilt. Such a delicate compromise they were all forced to accept;

all so aware of life's cruelest impulses, and yet they so desperately wanted to trust in the possibility of their renewal. But Adam gave them an alarming sense of the future. Everyone feared that something bad might one day happen to him, forcing them to recast all their hopes and dreams, start all over, amend their expectations.

The men of the colony—most of whom wished someday to have children of their own, or mourned the murdered children they left behind—took it upon themselves to act as surrogates for the Posners. The child was born and lived for most of the year in Brooklyn, but the refugees—many of whom lived in Brooklyn as well—committed themselves to year-round sentry duty. Even before Morris's illness, they undertook a shared communal responsibility to raise the boy.

Adam's actual father was never the kind of man well suited for the task, anyway. All the consolidated anguish of his life left him empty, distant, and cold.

Artie played catch with Adam. He even bought him his first baseball glove—a smooth black leather one with gold stitching and a Mickey Mantle signature. They would go out to the field and toss a pink Spalding back and forth. Artie was patient with some of Adam's erratic throws and his insistence on keeping the mitt sealed.

"Adam, open the glove," Artie would say. "You want to catch it, not knock it down!"

Morris watched from the porch, smiling and nodding occasionally—never once defying his doctor's orders. He had seen so much in his life—a great deal unspeakable and unknowable, particularly for those who existed outside the shared nightmare of Cohen's Summer Cottages. And he had come so far—as a boy in Germany; his early manhood in a concentration camp, and now, a withered and fading creature, unrecognizable to himself, spending his summers in the mountains of upstate New York, recuperating from a lifetime of distress.

Artie also taught Adam not to be afraid coming down on the slide.

"Just kick your legs through and slide."

"It's hot. I'll fall!"

"Come on, son, we've all been through worse than this, you can do it."

The bickering between Artie and Abe always came to a halt on account of Adam. On the days when Abe helped Adam build a kite from brown-paper wrapper, Artie refrained from polluting the otherwise buoyant air with lethal golf balls. In the end it didn't matter. Many a fruitless summer day passed without that reconstituted grocery bag ever getting off the ground.

Even Hyman Cohen himself helped out with the boy from time to time.

"Adam, follow me, *kind,* to the shed," he said, limping about. "We should find out the temperature for everybody."

Only five years of age, but Adam already knew the answer. He followed Cohen, and then obligingly emerged to announce: "It's eighty-five degrees!"

The last time anyone saw Morris was when Adam came running home from Krause's Cottages, crying and blowing on his wrist. Adam had been playing ball with the older boys. But they weren't throwing a soft Spalding. Adam must have been confused by the speed of their throws, or the weight of the ball. Artie's lessons didn't prepare him for life outside the colony. The children from the other edge of the forest didn't care about the *lager,* didn't reserve any special compassion for the boy with the sick father. The ball came too fast. Artie's glove didn't work.

The wrist was badly disfigured. A fleshy spike now occupied the place normally reserved for a pulse check. Panting away at the exposed bone, Adam thought only of how one soothes a burn.

"Phew, phew . . ."

He started to run, away from Krause's, in the direction of the rival colony that was his summer home. Dashing underneath the pines, through the woods, stopping every few steps to blow on the broken bone. As he got closer to the colony, he could make out the sight of his father sitting on the white porch, neat rows of picket columns off to each side. A watchtower connected to a bungalow, the only freedom Morris's doctor would allow.

Morris was sitting on an aqua beach chair, a crumpled German newspaper rested on the floorboards below him. He was perpetually on guard, expecting the worst—even here, so close to the otherwise calming influences of Kiamisha Lake. Adam reached the porch with a face filled with tears. Morris forgot all that his doctor had told him about stairs and the dangers of overexcitement. He pushed off the armrests, grabbed the railing, and then, as though he were a vital, solid man, raced down to his son.

"What happened to you, *mein sohn?"* he said, and hugged the boy as he had never done before. Adam held out his wrist—showing his father—staring down at it as though he had just brought home a wounded bird. "Oh, *mein Gott*—look at you . . ." And then, reflexively, with immediate regret, he let out, "Where can we be safe?"

Adam's lips trembled, and then, steeling himself, said, "Papa, you shouldn't have come down the stairs."

Morris embraced his son again, sobbing uncontrollably into the boy's small chest.

Moments later, a cavalry of refugees rushed to the Posner bungalow. Card games broke up suddenly. Wet laundry soaked in open baskets. A fishing pole lay dropped by the shore. No alarm had sounded, and yet somehow they knew to come. There was an intuitive sense that something was not right at bungalow 7. A people so sensitive to rescue, and the urgency to protect one of their fragile own.

"What happened?" old man Berman said.

"We came as soon as we saw the others start to run," one of the Jaffe brothers said, heaving desperately for air.

"Who is the sick one here?" Mrs. Kaplan wondered aloud. "Adam or Morris?"

Both father and son were taken to the hospital in Monticello, each in need of medical attention.

For weeks Morris lay in the hospital, connected to all sorts of life-sustaining machinery that couldn't possibly begin to heal what really ailed him. Rosa went off each day to Monticello to visit her husband. Adam, with his powdery white cast, was left in the care of one or several of the refugees, who were more than happy to do their part. There were rules at the hospital about not allowing visits by children. And after his experience with blanking out in that cold place—only to awaken with his arm fully recast in plaster—he had his own reservations about returning to the hospital as well. He wished to see his father, but only on the porch.

The bus edged up to the curb near the drugstore on Route 17, across the street from the bowling alley, just down the road from Cohen's. Up the other hill was the Concord Hotel. The door to the bus was open, the engine was running; the driver waited patiently for Rosa to get on.

"You be a good boy," Rosa said, brushing Adam's hair to one side. "Don't throw any more balls."

"I don't throw with my left arm."

"Then don't catch any more balls, and don't cause any more trouble."

She boarded, paid the fare, and slipped into the first seat. She then turned to the window to look back at her son. The bus pulled away. The roar and heavy exhaust seemed to smother the small boy. Adam remained behind, waving his heavy wrist.

With each afternoon return from Monticello, Rosa seemed different. She was edgier, more nervous than usual. Gradually she was saying good-bye to her husband—so unceremoniously, the awful finality so unjust. Each day Morris looked as though more of him had surrendered. There would be no going back to the bungalow.

Rosa would return, but never in the same way again. In sympathy with her husband's deterioration, her sanity began to leave her. She was losing her memory, her sense of place, her essential bearings, her grip on reality. Physically she was still strong, but the psychic toll had now become insurmountable—even for someone so seasoned in survival. Morris was leaving and ghosts were arriving. They took over her mind, ambushed her reason.

In what became an almost daily ritual, Rosa would retrieve her son and take him inside bungalow 7. Then the interrogation would begin:

"What did you tell the neighbors today?"

"I didn't tell them anything."

More forcefully. "What did you tell them?"

"Let go of my arm. . . ."

"Did you tell them about the box?"

"What box?"

"And the bullets?"

"What . . . ?"

"You told them about the bread, didn't you?"

"I don't know what you're talking about! . . . Mama, you're scaring me!"

"Tell me what you told them!"

She slapped Adam, who fell against the kitchen cabinet; the door panel slammed shut by the white cast. The crash caused a loud thud.

The child was too young to understand; the parent too mortified to concede the injury—to both of them.

Overwhelmed with grief, fatigue, and persevering nightmare.

It seemed like all those living near Kiamisha Lake descended on Cohen's Summer Cottages for the annual Labor Day bingo game. It started off as a bright and cloudless day. The temperature was cooling, fall was a few short weeks away. By then all the refugees would be gone, back to their respective boroughs, grateful that they had lived through another summer. Perhaps by next year, their memories of Europe would grow dimmer. But nobody actually believed that.

The bingo game was held outdoors on the grassy field. Long tables were set out. A sound system was installed to announce the numbers. People who had spent their summer traipsing from colony to colony in search of bingo by now felt fully practiced for the final game of the season—the World Series of bingo, the one with the biggest prizes.

"This is exciting," Adam said, slipping beside his mother in the last row, which was right in front of their bungalow.

Rosa was wearing one of her best dresses—a long beige sleeveless gown with a full-pleated bottom, a garment reserved for very special occasions. She was vastly overdressed—it was still summer, during the middle of the day, and hot—but nobody cared to notice. That's because there was so much else that could not be ignored. She had been given to walking around the colony late at night, howling into the woods like an animal. And, of course, there was her uncontrollable fury. Fortunately, the refugees knew to take care of her son on the days when her anger was directed at him.

"All these people," Adam continued.

Nursing his own two cards, Artie, who had become the closest thing that Adam now had to a father, sat next to him.

"I'd love to wallop a golf ball right into the middle of this place—that would get rid of everybody."

"The more people, the larger the pot," Rosa reminded him. She had instincts for these kinds of observations.

"Welcome to our end of the summer bingo tournament," Hyman announced from the podium with bravado. "The grand prize of two hundred dollars goes to the first person who can fill an entire card."

Rosa had waited all summer for this. She had a treasure trove of household trinkets to show for her preparation; now she was all geared up for the actual cash offerings.

"Mama, I have this card, right?" Adam asked.

"Don't bother me, I'm trying to concentrate."

She worked feverishly, tapping away at her cards.

"O twelve," Hyman's voiced screeched into the microphone. "I six."

"B thirty."

Rosa blotted the appropriate boxes, scouring the rows for the letters and numbers that would win her the title and bounty she so coveted.

Minutes into the game, Artie offered, "I got nothing. Must be a bum card."

"Shsh . . ." Rosa insisted.

They paid no attention to Adam, who was diligently filling in the boxes of his one card. He feared jinxing the outcome, so he kept the card to himself, hoping that neither Rosa nor Artie would notice the streak he was riding.

Some of the players had gotten up to walk around, moving slowly, mingling, drinking soda pop and eating sandwiches. A sharp, cool wind brushed over the colony, and a faint crackle of thunder echoed in the distance. Birds scattered from trees.

Adam slowly filled in the open spaces of his card—one at a time—as though he were working on a coloring book. Many of the other contestants appeared bored, tapping their fingers, waiting anxiously for a matching bingo ball to drop. Adam never noticed the collective frustration, or even the disappointment on his own mother's face, so uncharacteristic an expression for her to have while caught up in a game of chance.

All but one number had been filled on his card when the rains came. The afternoon summer shower drenched everything. Fortunately the bingo balls, made of wood, could float. As for the cards, streaks of Magic Marker smudged them beyond recognition, making them all indistinguishable. Cohen's Summer Cottages had been transformed into a finger-painting festival.

"This is the best my card is going to look," Artie said. "We should go inside."

"No!" Adam yelled.

"It's raining," Rosa said defeatedly. "We should go in. The game is over." Arms reaching toward the sobbing heavens, "What is wrong with my life! What did I do to deserve all this?"

"I have one number to go!" Adam screamed.

"Come . . ." Artie said.

The rain fell harder. All who had gathered for the afternoon now ran for the cover of the forest, or huddled under the roof of a bungalow, trying to outlast the downpour. Adam remained seated, alone on the bench. He stared at his solitary card, trying to shield it from fading, preserving the record of his unrealized triumph. Deprived of victory at his mother's favorite summer game.

"Bingo!"
"Bingo!"
"Bingo!"

A man with a thick, silver-speckled beard cried out for his prize, but no one responded.

It was fall in Sullivan County. Brown, red, and purple leaves looked vivid but fragile, about to surrender to the inescapable gravity that comes with autumn. Cohen's Summer Cottages were empty. Not at all unusual for that time of year. Not a living soul ever stayed at the colony past Labor Day. The place looked entirely different, but it wasn't the change in season that made it so.

It had been sold years before—the new name was not really important. The sign at the foot of the road had been replaced by something that had neither the wit, nor historical gumption, of LEISURE *MACHT FREI*.

He toured the barren grounds. The walking path was overrun with wild weeds and moss, the kind of unkempt, tangled growth that once colonized the former owner's eyebrows. The visitor surveyed the green field. He looked in the direction of the shed, and found nothing. When he got tired, he rested his back against the sinuous spine of that same weeping willow. It was still standing. The swings were gone, as was the slide. The ground was strangely moist, as though the earth had wept, or had never quite gotten used to the change in the landscape.

Looking back toward the bungalow—his old bungalow, 7—he watched as his son stood on an overturned pail. The boy needed a lift to see inside.

"Hey Mory, what are you doing? You'll fall down and hurt yourself! You might break your arm!"

The porch had been dismantled. The entrance was now supported by stilts. Plants uprooted. The entire place had been unearthed, barren, stripped of the emblems that once made it so familiar.

Slowly, Adam walked over to where his son was peering into the kitchen window, hands cupped along the side of his face like blinders.

"You see anything?"

"Not really. Just some old furniture moved up against the wall."

Adam took out his camera and snapped a picture of the boy on the pail. There was a sheriff's warning posted on the door.

AUTHORIZED PERSONS ONLY

" 'Authorized'?" Adam wondered. "If not me, who's allowed in then?"

But without the porch, how could you even enter? And once inside, what could you expect to find?

The camera clicked; he took a picture of the front door with the sheriff's sign on it. Ghosts, however, cannot be photographed. Those who he remembered would not sit still for a group picture. Only the sign would survive the eventual processing.

The colony had been transformed into a ghost town, which it had already been in a different way so many years before.

Mory turned around and jumped off the pail. Grabbing his father's hand, he ran off into the lifeless field, leaves crackling underneath each heavy step.

"So this was the place?"

"Sure is."

Looking up at the sky, hoping to pick up the sight of a brown paper kite, or a falling golf ball—some marking, something to pinch the senses and tweak the memories.

Some indication that the boy in the cast had once actually lived there.

"What are you looking for?"

"I don't know."

But he did.

"One number away from the jackpot, huh?"

"Yes. Never got the chance. Game called on account of rain."

"Bummer. Where's Krause's?"

"Over there. . . ."

THE
RABBI
DOUBLE-
FAULTS

The congregants of Temple Beth Am had long grown accustomed to the wayward antics of their spiritual leader. Rabbi Sheldon Vered, ordained in New York City but shipped off to Miami Beach in 1950, was a bit unorthodox even for someone who had already embraced Conservative Judaism.

The faculty at the Jewish Theological Seminary had banished him from the northeast. The collective opinion of the rabbis was that Sheldon Vered was "meshuga," perhaps suffering from sunstroke. So, like a child crated off to summer camp, Vered was assigned to South Florida, where, it was hoped, he could find a congregation that would better understand his condition.

No such luck.

Rabbi-about-town, dapper, handsome, with pressed silver hair that had the oily exterior of some tropical fish, glistening in the sun. The demands of his clerical life rested weightlessly on his shoulders, as though stoked by helium. Beardless and unscholarly, dressed in tapered Italian suits, he had long bony fingers with manicured nails. His pale blue eyes always seemed clear and untroubled, not at all capable of the kind of piercing, metaphysical investigations of an all-knowing rebbe. Fine rows of large capped teeth sparkled with an air of social confidence and position. He looked more the part of an investment banker than a deliverer of Old World reverence.

But the cosmetic ministrations did not end there. The rabbi was never without the deep, rich complexion of a devout Floridian, someone who well understood the limits of the First Commandment in the Sunshine State. Like all those who had forsaken the snowy sanctums of the north for the pagan customs of the golden tropics, Rabbi Vered was a worshipper of the almighty sun. God occupied a lesser role in the spiritual life of Florida's faithful.

"Nice shot, Rabbi," you could hear between points.

He was an avid and accomplished tennis player, a regular at all the neighborhood parks. Mistakenly he would schedule games on Saturday—during the service. Although a few hours late for his match, he would dash behind a curtain, disrobe, and reemerge with the twinkle of a child playing hooky, sneaking off to a remote court to make his appointment.

Fierce. Competitive. Unintimidated. Most of the time he played doubles, although occasionally he would hustle a younger foe, making sure to anchor the experience with a twenty-dollar bet on the side. He had that monstrous forehand smash, a high arching slam that smoked the asphalt and left skid marks in its wake. It was a lethal shot from any location on the court. With modern steel racket in hand, he was an uncharacteristically formidable opponent. Except for a black arm brace along the right forearm, he always wore immaculate all-white gear—from faddish toque to tennis shoes.

"You must have God flowing through that your right arm of yours, Rabbi," Manny Dubin, one of the neighborhood club players, would joke. "What's in that black arm brace, anyway? It's got to be either God or Rocket Rod Laver in there."

"The arm is my own," the rabbi would reply, "but if I had to choose between the two, I would pick Laver. His game I have seen. God's I have not."

Openly he boasted of having his way with the ladies—Jew and Gentile alike. Beautiful single women—many of whom half his age—took turns escorting the rabbi as he entered the ballrooms of hotels along Collins Avenue, making his grand appearance at the various ceremonies of his growing congregation. The biological and denominational imperatives that were mercilessly screened before one became a member of the synagogue were relaxed when it came to the rabbi's appetite for female flesh. He seemed genuinely unconflicted by tribal affiliations, dowry allotments, or the ability to keep a kosher home. There was even some talk of infidelities with married women—members of his own congregation, no less. A *shande* like this was unthinkable—even for him; so most people chose to focus their attentions elsewhere. The litany of allegations was so prevalent, it was best to just close your eyes and hope that the next morning's edition of the *Miami Herald* didn't have a front-page picture of Rabbi Vered embroiled in a sex scandal.

At bar mitzvahs and weddings, he refused to say the blessings over the wine and bread.

"It's not my job," he would say. "Get the grandfather to do it."

And once done performing the service, he simply took his place at the designated table; seated next to him, his date for the evening. He wanted no other part in the ceremony. A band would play a rhapsody of the long-forgotten but plaintive melodies of the Old World ghettos—a whiny clarinet, an awakened cymbal, a surging pulse of Yiddish harmony (*"Chiry bim, chiry bam, chiry bim, chiry bam, bim bam bim bam bim bam . . ."*); yet the rabbi remained at his seat. No twirling horas, no madcap spinnings with other males, not even a hoisting of the groom atop a chair. He was conserving his energy for later. When the musical mood had shifted—when repressed and neglected ancestral impulses had ceased to stir in the celebrants—he would rise with his date and run through a stirring fox-trot or a meticulous cha-cha. In later years, the floor would clear as everyone watched in amazement as the rabbi introduced his congregation to the twist, the pony, and a fairly upbeat mashed potato.

"This is a rabbi?" an occasional dissenter would exhort. "Where did we get this guy from, Peyton Place? A Cracker Jack box?"

"Yes, I'll admit, he is a bit eccentric," acknowledged a woman wearing a mink stole in August, "not at all like the rabbis from Brooklyn."

"Brooklyn! This person would be a disgrace in Iowa," another would join in. "A *mamzer*, I tell you. The old rabbis of Poland and Russia are turning over in their graves right now. Now *there* were rabbis. Ah yes . . ." humming himself into a trance, drifting into some nostalgic longing for those early stops along the Diaspora shuttle.

"Oh, please, this is America," came a different point of view. "We're in Miami for god's sake, not Odessa, not Lodz. We're about as far away from the pogroms, the Holocaust, and the Wailing Wall as you can get. We don't need the same kind of spiritual sustenance as we did in Europe. This man is fresh, new. You should be glad that we got us a modern rabbi."

"He's a goy—that's who he is!" An angry static of dissent pierced the debate. "We got us a heathen for a rabbi. We should call New York and get our money back. Isn't there a warranty that covers faulty rabbis? I'm sure there is." Then, blinking wildly, he added, "We might as well be led by Billy Graham—at least he's a personal friend of Nixon's."

A younger woman, as always, would rush to the rabbi's aid. "What do you want him to do—spend his entire life studying Talmud? Wear long black coats all the time? The man has nice legs, he should show them off. Besides, this is South Florida, the heat would kill him. We need a trim and fit rabbi who can take the humidity. The old-style rabbis would drop dead like flies. Better they should stay in Brooklyn."

"*Ach*, what do you know?" would come an elderly man's rejoinder. "America, a fake land. Nothing here is what it seems. They show you a statue of a lady holding a lamp when you first arrive. What does that tell you: Look where you're going."

Scattered protests like these were quite common, and understandable. Many were used to taking their religious medicine from old men who commanded the respect of the community by the force of their learning—not by their sexual conquests or the earnestness of their tans. Vered's flirtation with the secular world had angered those who remembered their rabbis as dark, shadowy figures; sullen, stoic, introspective, always ready with a life-sustaining parable or an elliptical portion of Talmud. Some regarded him as a phony cleric, an advance man for the venal impulses of the assimilationists, an impious dabbler of Scripture, a shameless dilettante faking membership in an ancient and honorable profession—as far removed from the Vilna Gaon as a rabbi could ever be. Not at all a man of God, but an exponent of corrupting godlessness; and worse than any goy because he was an apostate Jew.

So the old backbenchers of the synagogue braced themselves whenever Vered maneuvered his way to the pulpit. Like an exasperated chorus in a Greek tragedy, they observed the drama of their own spiritual decline with cynical disbelief, slapping their foreheads with each of the rabbi's passing indiscretions.

Those fiery sermons took on all the maddening flavor of a Southern evangelical tent show. Shouting and crying resonated throughout the sanctuary—not from cranky children or the spiritually overwhelmed, but from him. His fist pounding the air, he would migrate from pulpit to pulpit with great energy and determination, at times forcing the cantor to evacuate his own station—in fear of his life. A nap was impossible under such mounting turmoil. The congregation was forced to listen, and endure.

Despite questionable monastic credentials, the rabbi pontificated on all the subjects of the day: world affairs, cultural life, movies, art—and of course what mattered most to him and a large segment of his congregation—the destiny of the Miami Dolphins. The individual game-by-game statistics of Griese, Csonka, and Warfield rolled from his tongue like a hypnotic psalm.

"The line this week is the Fish by six points," he would announce from the pulpit, as the ark was about to be opened for the morning service. There was always understandable confusion about whether to turn the pages of the prayer books, or search for a copy of *Sports Illustrated*.

"So, my fellow former slaves, the point of this week's midrash is that Moses was the Bob Griese of his day. Both tremendous field generals. The game that Moses played against the Egyptians was not completely flawless—remember he did fumble the tablets and there was unnecessary roughness with that rock in the desert. But other than that, it was just like Griese's performance last season against the Bills. A real come-from-behind victory. The Jews had their backs against their own end zone—I mean here the Red Sea—and then," the rabbi dropping back as if about to throw a forward pass, "with split-second timing, Moses engineered a last-minute drive through the Red Sea and on to pay dirt—Canaan, of course."

Don Shula was once an invited guest for a Friday night service. Sitting next to the self-satisfied rabbi, Super Bowl rings attracting all sorts of overhead light, the coach seemed genuinely befuddled about what in the world he was doing at Temple Beth Am, and what, if anything, he was expected to say.

Fortunately, the rabbi was never at a loss for words, or clerical diversions. In such moments he would routinely fall back on some inanity. There was the time, early in his rabbinate, when he addressed the scandalous issue of marriages outside the faith.

"Today I would like to talk to you about the nominations in the best actor category for the Oscars. . . ." The sermon would begin, somehow winding its way to a conclusion: "The marriage between Eddie Fisher and Elizabeth Taylor is good for the Jews, just like Jacob's second wedding to Rachel."

A weary and dazed congregation would immediately search themselves for some possible Jewish meaning in all this. Heads turned in all directions. An occasional clue passed through the aisles, hoping to build into a thrust of clarity, gaining momentum, only to come to a disheartening halt. Resignedly, the congregation would conclude that, once again, there was just no explanation for the rabbi's methods. God works in mysterious ways; sometimes his servants follow the lead with equal inscrutability.

For a generally secular congregation, there was a fair amount of guilt over attending services that featured virtually nothing in the way of straight Scripture. Most of the service was conducted in English. When Hebrew was introduced, it was itself an occasion for celebration, and blessing. And what little Hebrew there was had been transformed. The melodies lost their Old World cantorial charm. Rather than the teary compositions that reflected the long-suffering travels of the Wandering Jew, Rabbi Vered had introduced the anthems of American show tunes and Tin Pan Alley classics as the musical backdrops for Hebrew prayers.

"What's wrong with it?" he asked, defending himself to those frequent doubters who accepted his reforms but longed for the mystical riffs of the past. Some wondered what else was being lost in the rabbi's flirtations with modernity. "The Gershwins are Jews. So is Irving Berlin. He wrote 'God Bless America.' Isn't that enough for you?"

As the times changed, so too did the melodies. The rabbi became partial to the sounds of Motown. The poor cantor, who had no choice in the matter, was instructed to lead the congregation in a medley from the Four Tops—the *"Adon Olam,"* given an altogether new, up-tempo arrangement, sung to the tune of "I'll be There."

And one day, as the hour grew late during a Yom Kippur service, Rabbi Vered let it slip that he had just eaten a tunafish sandwich. "What's a few hours? What harm can it do? I defy God to show his disapproval right now."

A few gasps and tremors, then awkward silence; finally, collective eyelids opened, a fearful peek at the pulpit to see if the rabbi had been turned to stone, or reduced to cinders.

The monument to irreverence that he set was still there. At best he was only penciled into the Book of Life.

Raising his arms in supplication, the rabbi proclaimed: "So you see. God is often impotent; or maybe he's out breaking his own fast. We have become a hypocritical people, and I, an appropriate leader for the times. We all attend services on the High Holy Days. We fast today. Or we claim to fast today. Keeping up the pretenses of a people who are no longer sure of the rules. We once had a god, but wandered as a lost tribe in search of a homeland. Now we have a homeland, but wander desperately in search of a god—some god, any god. Why are we here today? To make peace for the rest of the year in which we make war—in Saigon, in Watts, amongst ourselves, within our families? Because of fear? Most of you have already eaten. I know that, you know that. So what? God will not honor your fast—this much, as your rabbi, I know. Our connections are now strictly communal, no longer religious. We are the proud sculptors of golden calves. God has given us no reason to be otherwise. The world has shown us that there is nothing to fear from God—only ourselves. Go home and eat."

But one Saturday, to everyone's languid and unexpected wonder, the rabbi's image changed in the eyes of his congregation. There was a new understanding—leaving us unclear exactly of what to make of it at first—but nonetheless a sense that there was more to the rabbi's brand of Judaism than simply the mischief of a charismatic kook.

The rabbi walked somberly to the podium to begin his sermon and announced: "I am about to do something today that I have never done in all my years on the pulpit—allow someone to take my place, to deliver the sermon for today's service."

This animated all those who had gathered that morning. An ensemble of polyester slacks, pleated skirts, and fine hose brushed against the velvet seats of the synagogue, a stirring hum of alertness. The backbenchers perked up to attention, wondering whether the rabbi's gesture was, God willing, a signal of his impending resignation.

"But I would not relinquish my duties to just anyone. We have a special guest with us today. He is my brother. He is also a rabbi. He comes to us from Israel, where he leads his own shul. As children he and I never agreed on anything; we fought bitterly. The bible is filled with such brothers—Cain and Abel, Jacob and Esau, even Moses and Aaron."

The congregation was hearing many of these names for the very first time; the Bible was not generally a part of Temple Beth Am's Saturday curriculum. Today must have been a special occasion. Some members were actually taking down notes.

"Yet I know that my brother is a truly righteous man, a first-rate scholar, and a respected rabbi. Please welcome my brother, Rabbi Joseph Rose, from Tel Aviv."

No such thing as applause in a synagogue. Certainly not during a Saturday service, even in such a place where religious decorum had long given way to improvisational worship. People politely waited for the arrival of the rabbi's brother, wondering from what part of the sanctuary he would be making his entrance. At Temple Beth Am, he could have been dropped down by helicopter and no one would have thought the less of it.

Soon enough, out from behind a curtain, near the Plexiglas finished ark that was elevated high above the floor of the sanctuary, peered a man with a great ashen beard, a black robe, tiny spectacles, and a bloodless face. He walked down the stairs that led to the pulpit, nodded to his brother, and then stepped before the congregation. Hot overhead lights electrified his face, which was now imprisoned in a ball of fire, bringing his image closer.

The eyes of the congregation focused on the man before them, and then suddenly realized that this was not at all a new face. At first the association was difficult to make. You had to look behind the austere countenance, beyond the frailness of his carriage, teeth neither dazzling nor straight, the glasses and the beard. He looked like Rabbi Vered in disguise, minus a few weeks of the Florida sun—but in all other respects, he was clearly the rabbi's twin.

The guest rabbi looked over across the sanctuary, waiting for the right dramatic moment to begin.

"Good *shabos*," he said with an accent that was neither European nor Israeli, manufactured in the sands of ancestral dilution. "By now you must realize that Sheldon and I are twins, identical ones. As a child I always felt that he was the better-looking of the two. Now I am sure of it. You have, as they say, a movie star for a rabbi. In such a country this must be an advantage. My brother, Rabbi Robert Redford."

A murmur of uneasy laughter rose from the sanctuary, then died down immediately, as though signaling a false alarm. Backbenchers whispered amongst themselves—plotting some strategy to swap rabbis, working out a deal with Tel Aviv—already satisfied that the twin was a vast improvement.

Rabbi Joseph Rose spoke eloquently and calmly for nearly an hour. He covered the text in the Torah, cited the Talmud, referred to the biblical passage of the day—which just happened to be about Joseph, the one with the fancy coat, and the *tsouris* with his own brothers; and to the astonishment of his mesmerized lot, sprinkled Hebrew around liberally. The parched but grateful congregation received his words as though he were speaking a new language.

And as if his scripted performance was not numbing enough, there was an ad-lib revelation that would change Temple Beth Am forever.

"Before I leave you on this day, I would like to say a few words about my brother." Rabbi Vered looked on from his exalted high-backed chair, seated ten feet away, next to the cantor. "This is, as you say here in America, a reunion for my brother and me. In over thirty years we have not seen each other. I left Poland as a young man, a Zionist, to become a pioneer in Palestine. That was in the year 1936. A few years later the Nazis came and destroyed the life that we knew as children. Our parents were killed, and our older sister, Miriam, too. I don't know if Sheldon has told you this, but he was taken to Auschwitz. He survived, but only after years of hard labor in the rock piles—like an animal, smashing away at rocks. Not since Egypt had the Jews suffered this much cruelty. My twin brother, so smart and educated, always the most brilliant one in school, the most serious, filled with the most passion for learning, for God. Reduced to smashing tremendous rocks with a great hammer, turning them into small stones.

"I feel guilty over the different paths that we were to take. For me it came by accident. I ran away from an Orthodox home. Our father, Moishe, wanted both Sheldon and me to become rabbis. I wanted instead to become a political man. Palestine meant freedom, a new life. I abandoned my father, and God. Sheldon, the prize of our yeshiva, would not leave. God needed him too much.

"After the war was over, I learned what had happened to our family. The people at the refugee center told me that Sheldon died in Auschwitz. Only recently I learned that he is alive and living here in Florida, as your rabbi. It's a funny story how I came to find this out. I was walking in Tel Aviv. I saw a tourist with a copy of the *Miami Herald.* There was a picture of a face. It looked a little like my face. I asked to see the paper, and there was Sheldon, dressed in a tuxedo, a picture of him, smiling, with a tan, standing next to a young woman. They were at a charity event. Sheldon never tried to find me, but I found him by looking at the society column of your paper. And here I am.

"After the war, from guilt and the knowledge of the murders done to our people, I decided to return to God. I studied to become a rabbi after all, which would have made my father happy and proud. I live in a country where we must reconcile the obligations of a Jew who is forced to carry a gun. The job of the rabbi is always to give his congregation a sense of God's presence.

"My brother had to learn to endure so much, it is a wonder that he also decided to honor our father's wishes, and to fulfill his own destiny by becoming a rabbi. Like twins separated at birth, we have, on our own, without any interference, become the same.

"I am curious to know the kind of rabbi he has become. After what he has seen, where could he lead you but to a house of mirrors? You must forgive his sadness, the sense of rage he must feel. Auschwitz can't help but affect the way he chooses to introduce you to God. Your rabbi must be filled with such bitterness, such anger, such confusion—how does he explain this all to you, to make sense of this world, allowing you to order your lives with meaning, and with a sense of God's eternal presence?"

Stiffly, awkwardly, the congregation squirmed with the knowledge that Rabbi Joseph Rose didn't know his brother. The twins were not the same.

"Good *shabos,* everyone."

The next day, the rabbi telephoned our apartment—looking for me. Never before had he called our home. My bar mitzvah had taken place a few months earlier; not that he would have bothered to notice, or remember. That wasn't why he called. My successful rite of passage alone would not have roused him into checking on my progress as a newly minted member of the tribe.

I was right.

My mother stood nervously at the foot of my room, holding the telephone receiver with one hand, muffling the bottom end with the other, and whispering as though the police were standing outside. There was a happy glow to her face. If I didn't know better, I would have assumed that she had just received a blessing from Southern Bell.

"I think the rabbi wants for you to play tennis with him," she said excitedly. "He asks if you are playing with anyone else today. *Oy gotinyu,* I knew this day would come."

I had been playing junior tournament tennis since I was ten years old, winning a few trophies here and there, traveling the state of Florida—from Key West to Tallahassee—with a sober eye toward my rankings. Rabbi Vered was always looking for a good game. I would have remained anonymous to him—safe from his grasp—had he not seen that picture of me at South Shore Park, holding up a trophy nearly twice my size. With both hands I lifted the thing—the sleek figurine resting on top, the bronzed outline of a perfect serve. The trophy was so big you could hardly see my face in the photo. Underneath, the caption read:

ADAM POSNER, OPTIMIST CHAMPION.

It was my first big tournament win, and it inspired the rabbi to take a renewed interest in me—not as a Jew, but as a fourth.

To my parents, Saul and Ruth, forever creatures of the fallen Europe, Rabbi Vered was a hero. They were charmed exactly by what the backbenchers loathed. The rabbi as sinner, religious deviant, violator of commandments, diluter of ritual, thumber of God. During all those years that he played the role of the rabbinic fool, they soaked up the sacrilege. There were those who had hoped that the rabbi would somehow reform himself, in time out-grow the rebellion and slip placidly into the stereotype. Not my parents. The more anarchy the better, privately applauding his irreverence. Like feckless bystanders witnessing a riot, they wished for the rabbi to continue shaking the celestial rafters of God's silence. They preferred the tennis-playing, women-chasing, sun-worshipping rabbi—secretly egging him on, encouraging even greater lapses from tradition and piety.

They only wished they could do the same—as a punishment to God, as a symbol of justified disobedience.

And now, after the brother's sermon, they were even more en-amored of him. He was one of them. A survivor too. They could understand him better—the real rabbi, not the cardboard carica-ture. But they were also rendered somber, contemplative; the knowledge of the affliction they shared with the rabbi had ruined the presumed simplicity of his dissent. His madness was their madness—nothing less. He wasn't simply a joker or a comedian, mocking God just for laughs. Rabbi Vered was responding in some deeply human way to what he had witnessed. His method was crude and curious, and one wondered whether it even worked, but he had taken a crucial step forward, into the void of the living, where his scream, if not understood, at least resonated as lunacy. If only my parents could have found a therapy of their own—even one as equally pointless and defeating.

The congregation of Temple Beth Am had been treated to new gossip about a man once thought to be uncomplicated, but now seemingly more complex than anyone would have ever imagined.

"Adam, you must speak to the rabbi."

Taking the phone, I heard the rabbi say, "Adam, my boy, I have a bar mitzvah present for you."

"My bar mitzvah was two months ago."

"So I'm a little late."

"What is it?" I asked cautiously.

"You can play a game of doubles with me today. My brother

says he can play. I'll find us a fourth. How does that sound to you?"

"Can I have something else?"

"Don't *hondel* with me. I'm the rabbi. Meet me at the courts at three."

I returned the receiver to my mother, who then asked, "Well? Was I right?"

"He wants me to play doubles with him today. He's bringing his brother, you know, the man from yesterday."

"How wonderful," my mother said, both her hands occupied in caressing her large, soft face. "In between two rabbis my boy will play."

"It's not a sandwich, Mom, just doubles."

"You told him you'd be there, didn't you?"

"I didn't have time, he hung up before I could answer."

"You can't pass up such an opportunity. Think what you could learn."

A stiff silence wedged in between us as she contemplated my good fortune, and I wondered how my tennis game could possibly improve through the intervention of dueling clerics.

"I don't think I want to go. They'll mess up my game. Playing with those guys is like Ping-Pong; it's too slow."

"Adam, he's the rabbi, don't forget."

"So?"

"If our rabbi wants to play tennis with you, it's an honor. A respected man he is in the community."

"That's not what most people say."

"You heard what his brother said yesterday: his history, we share. He knows what we went through. In a way you are related to him."

I pondered the newly discovered bond, unsure of how the rabbi, implausibly, overnight, had become a relative.

Sensing that I wasn't making any of the right connections in her plea, my mother paused to find some other solicitation, and concluded, "Do you not want to be a good Jew, Adam?"

"What does playing tennis with the rabbi have to do with being a 'good Jew'?"

"I hear he's a good player."

"I hear he cheats."

"Adam, you cannot say such things. Who knows, God may be watching."

"Good. I hope he'll be keeping score."

Hours later I was off to the courts with my racket hanging in a sling along my neck. It was early afternoon. The sun was far back in the open sky. The air thick, choking, stripped of vitality. By the time I arrived, the rabbi and his brother were already playing on center court.

The brothers were warming up, hitting the ball back and forth over the net: a streak of curving white fuzz lifted from the ground and then bounced over the other side with great, looping arches.

Although identical twins, the brothers were easy to tell apart. It wasn't just the uncoordinated beard and the pale white legs that confounded their otherwise obvious biological ties; it was the manner of their play, as well. Our rabbi was given to aggressive and punishing hits; a furious and aching grunt would coincide with each stroke of his steel racket. The Israeli Rose, by notable contrast, was more calm and methodical in his approach to the game, preferring placement and strategy to sheer brute force.

The times made it impossible not to admire the Israelis for their courage and cunning in the face of hostile enemies. So it came as a shock to see a Miami Beach rabbi attacking the ball as if a war were going on, and his brother, an unusually tame Israeli, playing under conditions of a cease-fire.

The Holocaust is the great equalizer of stark interior dramas: reordering nerves, creating strengths and exploiting frailties, transforming individuals into something they would not have otherwise been. I was too young to realize that then.

I sat on the lawn, watching, hoping that perhaps they would decide to go it alone, play a fraternal game of singles and leave me, an only child, out of their sibling rivalry. But that was not to be. Soon they walked over to my side of the court, wiping off their lathered foreheads and racket handles with terry cloth.

The rabbi said, "Ah, finally, here at last. I am anxious to see you play."

"So this is the young prodigy," his brother said, extending his hand for a warm, friendly shake. "I am your rabbi's brother. Please call me Joseph."

"I know who you are," I said. "I heard your sermon yesterday. I'm Adam." And then reflexively, as though guided by my mother's needy, desperate soul, I added, "My parents were in the camps too." Spoken as some secret password, a sacramental wink that just might confer immediate acceptance into the brotherhood of those related to survivors of the Holocaust.

Shaking his head, Rabbi Vered said, "I didn't know this about your parents."

The Israeli brother paused, and said, "Nice to meet you, Adam. It must be difficult to be their son. You are their one hope, their answer to the world. They are living through you. A difficult burden for a young boy, I'm sure. Maybe this explains all of those tennis trophies, no?"

"I don't know," I replied haltingly. "Never really thought about it that way. They're not like other parents, that's for sure. Much more nervous, you know, scared. Hard to feel safe around them."

A certain, palpable fear rose in me. Childhood defenses knew not to focus on these matters too much; best to cloak them with sunny diversions. But now, on the tennis court—the place of my habitual refuge—my true age had betrayed me. Typical of sun-stroked Florida, the skin of these rabbis' pasts were about to peel away, and they were about to strip me bare with them.

"Poor boy," Joseph said. "I can imagine."

Rabbi Vered interrupted hastily, "Maybe the two of you should play together. You have come to America find a brother, Joseph; maybe you have found one in Adam."

Apparently the brothers had not slept all that well the night before. So many years unaccounted for, they were forced to compress their homecoming, and their consolidated grievances, into a short time span. No fraternal roughhousing that might have gone on. No dissipation of the feud. They awoke the next morning not at all closer, but rather filled with the curious need to whack a tennis ball around.

All those years that Sheldon could have attempted to locate his brother in Israel, and didn't. Joseph, forced to live with the knowledge that he had abandoned his martyred family, fortuitously learns that his twin is alive and well, cavorting in Miami Beach—eating unkosher food, sleeping with forbidden women, mocking God. The silver prince of the city, turning back the clock and outrunning his memories as if life was devolving in reverse.

"Why must we continue this?" Joseph implored. "I thought we could find peace on the tennis court."

"I don't think there can be any sanctuary for this kind of quarrel. We are different people. We now live different lives. I have seen what you cannot possibly ever know, and that knowledge sets us apart, has changed the biological fact that we are brothers. I have seen madness, not abstract biblical madness, but the real thing, man to man, monster to man. It is impossible for us any longer to share the same sensations. The world has been turned on its head, and when such things happen, having a twin is not such a big deal."

"God help us . . ."

"I was right," the rabbi continued. "The two of you would make a good team. Adam, you can serve the ball and Joseph here can pray for victory. In such a cockeyed world, these prayers God might answer."

"Sheldon, not in front of the boy."

"Why not in front of the boy? Let him think for himself. Make up his own mind about his God, whether to even have a god."

"Are you speaking now as his rabbi, or as a bitter Holocaust survivor?"

"Why does it matter? My eyes are open—no matter which hat

I wear. There is no escape from life. And I resent being called 'bitter.' I am not bitter, on the contrary, no one experiences life with my passion. Adam will tell you that, even he knows."

"It is ironic to me that this is the kind of spiritual meaning you chose to give to your congregation."

"My job is not to give 'spiritual meaning,' " the rabbi shot back, "but life lessons. The world does not need more ways to understand God. It is a lost cause. God," he chuckled, "if there even is a god, has shown that he, or she, is unknowable, incomprehensible, an abstraction with a dangerous sense of humor. Job sat on a pile of shit and God told him not to question. Our entire family was murdered. I am not so obedient."

The rhythmic movement of this debate had the lobbing sensation of the game we were about to play. God as abstraction? God as bouncing ball? What I did know was that God had been an ambivalent presence in my home. The Holocaust survivors who were my parents wanted to hate God, wished to hold Him responsible for their senseless suffering and his unintelligible silence, but the Jew in them made such mutinies of the heart impossible. That was a luxury for those not imprisoned by fear and tradition. A silent God in times of madness is frightening, but even that is better than no God at all. Because even at these times when the world seems more hopeful and composed, there is the need to feel that the planet is not set adrift within the blackened cosmos. The rabbi was unconflicted by such anxieties; it made him more comfortable in his obsessions.

Shaking his head, Joseph said, "I cannot believe you are a rabbi."

"Who sent you? Did you travel all this way to convert me? I suggest you find another way to rid yourself of guilt. You want me to find God? Too late. I am a godless rabbi. Unusual, yes, but that's my calling. I have found life, instead! You speak as a rabbi who knows God but doesn't. I don't speak of God because I'm afraid I do know him."

"*Shah* still! Enough already with this!" a snarling voice entered the fray.

The fourth had finally arrived. Morty Kaplan, a balding sharpie with perpetual beads of sweat clinging to his face, dropped a can of tennis balls on the court in hopes of provoking a truce. By trade, Morty was the owner of The Jewish Nostra, a Miami Beach delicatessen, which wasn't, by any standards, a typical Jewish deli. The place was packed all day long with numbers runners, bookies, overweight thugs, shady accountants, and just about anyone on the Beach who had ties to the local Jewish syndicate. Even with the best corned beef south of the Rascal House, rarely did you ever see a retiree or snowbird eat there, or even order take-out. A potato knish, even a good one, was not worth the risk of such associations.

He was also a close friend of the rabbi, dragging him along to the dog track and jai alai. They also had a regular poker game on Thursday nights with a few cigar-chomping Flushing transplants, all of them breathing, miraculously, through uneven noses. "Have we come here to play tennis, or discuss philosophy?" he asked. "The two of you haven't seen each other in all these years, and all you can do now is fight over God?"

"There's no fight," the rabbi said. "When it comes to God, I will let my brother win."

Resignedly, Joseph exhaled deeply, and conceded, "Perhaps you are both right. I apologize. I have come here hoping to accomplish too much. I tried to find my brother, but I also wanted to become his keeper, and to save his soul. I have no right to do that."

"It is also too late," the rabbi said. "The time for that has long past."

"The time is tennis," Morty pleaded. "We have the court only for an hour. Are you all warmed up?"

"Sheldon and I hit a little earlier."

"How about you, kid?" Morty said, looking at me, dripping a few suds of perspiration on my head.

"I haven't been on the court yet," I replied shyly, my voice cracking a little, my face overridden with acne.

"You're young, you'll warm up as you play."

"What are we playing for?" the rabbi inquired.

"What do you mean?" Joseph wondered.

Pausing, trying to break the news gently, I said, "I think your brother wants us to bet something if we lose."

"I never play a game without a friendly wager," the rabbi informed his quizzical sibling.

"Of course not," Morty intervened. "Who would?"

"Are they joking?" Joseph said, staggered at how little he knew his own twin.

"I don't think so. I think they're serious."

"I like the stakes from here," Morty said, rubbing his chin with a sinister smile. "How about the usual? Fifty bucks, two out of three sets. How much you got in your pocket, kid?"

I started to reach inside my tennis shorts, and said, "Uh . . ."

"That won't be necessary, Adam," the rabbi said, to my relief. "We won't play for money, not this time."

"Of course not," added his brother, "it would be a *shande*, two rabbis playing for money. And don't forget there is a child involved."

"That's no child," Morty said. "The kid's a ringer, and he was bar mitzvah a month ago. He's a man; he can bet." Turning to the rabbi: "Sheldon, what do you mean we won't play for money? We always play for money. Come on, can't we play for money? I just went to the bank to get cash. . . ."

Rabbi Vered had come to some Solomonic solution. "No, I think a bet is proper here, but the stakes will not be measured in cash. We should play for something else."

"What else is there?" Morty asked, annoyed and incredulous at the same time. "You want them to write a check?"

"I don't like the way this sounds," Joseph said.

"I have a way to make this interesting," the rabbi mused. "My brother, the true believer, this is what I propose: If Morty and I win, you will have to introduce a healthy dose of skepticism into your services. God can no longer be the Almighty—but rather at times you should refer to him as an absent God, or a vacationing God. I won't ask you to remove God from your congregation's life, but you will have to show a different side of God, the one that I have seen. As for you Adam, you will have to play me a game of singles once a week for an entire year."

"What do I get out of this?" Morty turned to his rabbinical friend, blinking inquisitively.

"You may have to sit this one out, Morty," the rabbi said. "You'll play, but no reward. As a favor to me. I'll make it up to you."

"Ah, I see," Joseph said, a nervous but admiring gleam in his eye. "But what if we were to win?"

"Choose your prize," the rabbi suggested.

Years of estrangement, unresolved guilt, and seething resentment had made the brothers strangers to one another. Joseph Rose had been insufficiently acquainted with his twin to know the sacred truths that the rabbi would have the most difficulty relinquishing.

I grabbed the hem of Joseph's shirt and dragged his head down to my mouth while I whispered in his ear. He smiled and nodded exuberantly. "I think Adam has come up with something that would satisfy our team. The members of Temple Beth Am have been deprived long enough. Perhaps this is the true purpose of my mission after all. So, these are our terms: If we win, Sheldon, you will have to bring God back into the synagogue. You will have to open the Torah, and read from it too. Rather than delivering long-winded sermons about the Whales . . ."

"The Dolphins, Joseph."

"Why yes, of course, the Dolphins, Nancy Sinatra, Richard Nixon, and *The Jackie Gleason Show*. You will be required to introduce more prayer back into the service, the old hymns—the *Ashray* and *Yigdal*—and not more of that crazy Beatles music that Adam tells me about."

"Hey, how do I get in on some of this action?" Morty wondered. "You can't ask me to play without some percentage."

Everyone ignored Morty. With a baiting smile, Rabbi Joseph Rose asked: "*Nu*, do we have a game?"

"So we play for God," the rabbi said, steely eyed, fixed on his brother.

The afternoon sun blazed like an oven. Clouds drifted in from the Atlantic. A stiff, muggy breeze faded in and, almost as quickly, out. I pondered the stakes that I had created. A victory would change our synagogue forever. And I could help make that happen. Who knew whether the entire congregation would have welcomed such a return to the old ways of religious observance. They had become so accustomed to Rabbi Vered's bastardized pietism. After over twenty years of marching to the psalms of a different, perhaps demented, drummer, who was I—only recently bar mitzvah—to shift us all in radical directions, back under the sway of ritual, into the cave where sleep the vagabonds of our vanished faith? It might seem pleasing to a few backbenchers, but what about everyone else? Under whose authority was I operating?

And what if we were to lose? I, the tennis prodigy, consigned to a special brand of purgatory: fifty-two matches with Rabbi Vered over the year. Forget my tournament career and the maintenance of my already fragile ranking. Might as well retire and clip hedges, or treasury-bond coupons. And what about Rabbi Joseph? Such a nice man would be forced to convert his synagogue—make it more like ours. Fresh from manhood—as a first act of Jewish responsibility—I had been given the power to transform Temple Beth Am into a true house of God. With the same act, I might also be able to accomplish what a Jeremiah could not—rescue an innocent shul from the Sodom and Gomorrah that we had become.

God as the trophy? Me as redeemer? My parents really would have been proud.

Rabbi Vered started to reapply some Coppertone fast-acting tanning oil, rubbing it all over his face, over his legs, then along the left arm; the right arm was already busy with the black brace. He then said, "We'll take this side."

"Your eyes will be in the sun," I reminded him.

"We'll switch after every two games," Joseph said.

"Who's switching?" the rabbi roared. "Not me! You stay on the other side. In the shade, in the dark, where you belong."

The teams took their respective sides. Rabbi Vered and Morty served first. The rabbi perched himself in front of the net. His enormous smile mirrored the sun as though his punishing ground strokes were not enough of an advantage on their own. Morty was warming up at the baseline. A pudgy mass of perspiring flesh, bending from side to side, swinging his racket as though swatting imaginary flies. Behind him, the green-mesh canvas that bordered the fence, absorbing the light, enveloping us as though the court was the home of an Orthodox ritual bath.

The game was off to a fast and furious start. The rabbi and Morty had played tennis together before. They had a sense of each other's movement, knowing when to call for the ball, and when to let it go. The choreography of their game was impressive. Two older fellows hustling around the court, switching positions, diving when necessary. Morty's consistent play was inexplicable on a day when money was not on the line. The lure of a bet had in the past propelled Morty and the rabbi to feats of athletic excellence that a regular game could not possibly ever inspire. His loyalty to the rabbi now must have acquired a new, special urgency.

After falling to a quick 4–2 deficit, Rabbi Joseph and I started to work our way back. Because of my youth and speed, I played the baseline, chasing down one slice and lob after another, while Joseph prowled the net—where the rabbi roamed on the other side—facing his brother down with hotly exchanged volleys.

"That was out," the rabbi said, pointing south, away from our court. We had just dropped another game.

"Sure looked good to me," I mumbled, and then, huddling with my teammate, I said, "I hate to say this, Joseph, but I think your brother, my rabbi, cheats. I heard it was true, now I see for myself."

"You noticed it too," he said.

"But he's a rabbi," I said innocently. "He can't cheat. Don't they teach you guys sportsmanship over at the yeshivas? In my junior high school, Coach Kucholokas would make us run laps for cheating in a game."

"This has nothing to do with him being a rabbi," Joseph said somberly. "My brother's behavior—all of his behavior—is a challenge to God. Sheldon has been long lost. In the camps he had to learn how to survive. He never cheated in school as a boy, but all that changed him. He learned to become ruthless, untrusting, mercenary. Survival is a game of winning and losing. He learned how to win. We are now playing according to his rules. This is not your usual opponent, Adam. You are playing tennis on this side; on that side, who knows what he thinks he is playing—many different games at once, I suppose. Unfortunately, he is just a survivor who hasn't learned that neither this game, nor the synagogue, are part of that other world, where he learned to play this way."

"All right, stop the conferencing over there," Rabbi Vered shouted from across the net. "What's going on? You two discussing strategy? It won't help you. Say your prayers—you're mine."

A can of balls was scrapped for a new one. Rabbi Vered complained that the old ones had lost their vitality, which may have been true. Even I was forced to admit that he made a tennis ball wish for a softer existence; the rabbi hit harder than anyone I had every played against. That forehand smash of his resonated like amplified thunder; the strings of his steel racket seemed to collapse with each stroke, turning his weapon into a butterfly net. But all that rage and tenacity gave rise to erratic mistakes.

"Way to go, Joseph," I screamed, after a particularly smooth return that nearly clipped the rabbi's hair, forcing him to duck. "That ties it up, one set apiece."

The brothers seemed to be gunning for one another. "Should I have taken out an extra insurance policy for this game?" Morty wondered. "Things are getting pretty hot here. Maybe we should take a break and cool the two of you off a little. I'll go and get us all some orange soda."

"No breaks," the rabbi said. "We play to the end."

"It's just a game, Sheldon," Morty persisted. "We're going to have to carry one of you out on a stretcher."

"Clouds are coming," the rabbi warned. "If we don't keep playing, we won't finish the match."

"He's right," Joseph said.

Could it be possible that Morty, the unapologetic confidant of gangsters, and I, were the only sane ones in South Shore Park that day? Perhaps it was just that the stakes were ultimately meaningless to us; while for the brothers, God was indeed watching, as my mother had wisely suspected.

"Come on, your serve," the rabbi urged.

That last set was memorable. A crowd of spectators had edged themselves close to the court, sharing a collective sense that this was no ordinary match. The four of us had anxious looks on our faces, and a complete absence of humor. An undefined purpose other than recreation had taken hold of the final set.

We traded points and games. Deuces took an eternity to mediate. Legs began to cramp, and fatigue set in like the tide off Biscayne Bay. Even I became winded, which said much for the determination and grit of my older colleagues. At 5–5, we decided to play a tiebreaker.

The rabbi had been right about one thing: the skies had become dark—bruised purple clouds, puffy black cotton eyes, marshaled overhead like an idle army. You could see the far-off ripple of gray light, and hear the swelling thunder, rumbling like a heavenly landslide. Miami's customary summer warning of a game about to be interrupted.

"Whoever gets seven points first wins," the rabbi announced. "Get ready to lose."

He was right again. The man knew something about psychological warfare—learned in the most experimental of trenches—where the immediacy of last-set heroics represented something that couldn't be measured in a Davis Cup. Morty just stood by as a spectator, the top of his racket suspended on the asphalt. The rabbi served and volleyed, placed the ball with perfection, slammed it down with authority.

Five unanswered points later, it was his service. The first ball collided into the net, pushing it forward like a windblown sail. "Fault!" he yelled. The sky darkened even more. A cool breeze came in from the ocean. The next serve sliced through the air and found a spot on the court from which no return was possible.

"Ace!"

"We're in trouble," I said.

But Joseph was looking over at the other side of the court, back at the baseline, where his brother was staring downward in terror. The last serve had unleashed not just the ball, but the rabbi's arm brace, which, propelled by all that fury, was also thrown forward to the net.

"What is it?" I asked.

Morty approached his teammate slowly, leaning down to retrieve the brace. The rabbi stared at his own uncovered right arm. The fallen brace revealed the rabbi's numeric tattoo—162014—his identity in the camps. Naked on the court. Indelible, irreversible stain—all that he had become. The rabbi flinched at the sight of his own exposed flesh.

"Here you go, Sheldon," Morty said tenderly. "Put it back on."

Silence. The sky stayed momentarily calm.

"No, I play without it this time."

Nervously, Morty continued, "Are you sure, Sheldon? You always have it on. It's match point."

"Your service!" the rabbi yelled out to us.

"Go ahead, Joseph," I said. "Backs up against the wall. Hope I haven't let you down."

But Joseph was unable to move. Eyes still fixed on his brother. His beard flapped a bit in the quickening wind.

"Are you all right?" I asked hesitantly. "Everyone's watching. It's time to serve."

Without saying a word, he walked back to the service line, lifted two balls from the court, and positioned his angular body into that twisted choreography that begins the travels of a tennis ball.

The first ball limped fraily without much speed or height, and teetered against the net. I had been taught by coaches to anticipate the moment of victory, to feel it, to imagine it before it even happened. And now the same clarity would set in—even in a loss. There was silence everywhere—the crowd, the skies. Everything seemed to slow down from its original pace.

Joseph tossed the ball into the air and guided his racket. With more force this time, the ball once again tangled itself in the net, and dropped like a conquered fish.

The rabbi raised both his arms in victory. Morty ran toward us with an extended arm. A tremendous crack of thunder split the heavens; everyone ran for cover underneath the concession stand.

The rabbi remained alone on the court. The rains came. Thunder noisily echoed throughout Miami Beach, sounding the drumbeat of defeat, the ancient rhythm of celebration, and rage. With eyes closed and a hand atop his head—the other swinging above his shoulder—the rabbi moved gracefully into a Hasidic dance, mumbling Hebrew words of revelation, spinning joyously in the luminous rain.

LOST,
IN A
SENSE

There was no way of explaining it, certainly not then, not now—never. We were children, running shirtless and carefree. The times were different, uncomplicated. Our peeling bronzed skin crackled in the sun, the signature of solar exuberance. What did we know? We were imprisoned by a sense of invincibility. Our youth demanded as much. Those complacent smirks, those knowing winks; the passion behind each impulsive strut.

It was all a game of hide-and-seek with the sun. But one day the sun didn't return, and the eclipse never left us.

In less than a year everything, and I mean *everything,* changed.

I remember when I first met Brad. The fall when the Mets had just won the World Series. I was nine years old. He was eight. We resided in Miami but rooted for franchises with Yankee refinements. Despite our Florida sunburns and year-round cabana attire, neither of us had lost any of our allegiance to New York sports teams. We were dispossessed, with longing devotion, championing the cities, and teams, of our birth.

And so there I was, throwing a beaten tennis ball against the side wall of the Point, setting up a regular pattern of bouncing thumps that annoyed a few old men who were reading newspapers by the pool. I was testing my arm, and my imagination, against an invisible batter with Major League credentials. And as if the heat were not enough to intimidate my foe (and here I speak of the relative strength of my arm, not the weather), my face was smeared a ghostly white, caked with the tribal war paint of zinc oxide, applied compulsively by my parents.

Unlike their American contemporaries, my parents had witnessed firsthand the misfortunes that imperil the unprotected. The tragedy that destroyed their lives years earlier provoked an abundance of caution in all things. Without really knowing the science behind the sun, they assumed its unquestioned bad faith. It caused us to squint our eyes, which exaggerated already distorted biases. It burned our skin under the pretense of vigor. And for those who tanned, it fueled isolated conceits and dark vanities. My parents armored their son against these undisguised elements.

"And here we are, ladies and gentleman. The final game of the World Series," I announced. "Bottom of the ninth, two out, and the Mets are up three–two against the Orioles. *Hrrrr. . . .*" I mimicked the sound of a roaring crowd, until Brad showed up, the new kid on the island.

"Who are you supposed to be?" he asked.

"Jerry Koosman," I replied, taking a time-out during my rotation. It was my game after all, and baseball is inherently timeless—a well-suited sport for our island. The relocated crowd from Shea Stadium was kept in a cruel suspense.

"All I see is a kid with bird shit on his face."

And that's how the friendship began. I never even pitched to that last batter. I just dropped the ball and walked away, leaving a weightless Boog Powell scratching his head, wondering how it would all turn out.

Within moments we exchanged names. We revealed our deepest secrets with that capacity only children have to disarm all the doubts and suspicions that haunt adult relations.

We dove into the swimming pool, that pale green basin that offered momentary respite from the brutal heat. All this was undertaken inside the reflection of Matt's Ray•Ban sunglasses. Matt was the Point's lifeguard. Muscular and tan, he had dirty blond hair, which served as a sponge for chlorine and sweat.

"Stay out of the deep end!" he would yell, those perfunctory warnings never reaching us. His voice drowned inside the ripples of our submerged adventures.

Air bubbles floated to the surface, followed by our gasping lungs. After replenishing our oxygen, we would plunge down to the bottom of the pool and lift the hatch that covered the drainpipe. We thought we were unleashing the treasures of the Spanish Armada—ancient coins, golden amulets, enough silver to bulge the eye of a pirate right through his patch. We did not consider it such a historical anomaly, after all. As children of Florida, we learned of the great Spanish conquistadores who once roamed the state in search of gold and the salvation of Indians. Ponce de León may have himself guessed that our island might someday attract the ever young and promiscuous. The foundation for the Fountain of Youth was right under our feet.

Miami in those days was a tropical Oz, minus the dueling witches. Bright colors, a tireless sun that left its imprint of mugginess everywhere—even at night. Palm trees swayed like the skirts of island maidens. Boats rocked gently from side to side, anchored in a maze of marinas. Others coasted through canals into the deepest and most calm of blue waters. A dreamy paradise set adrift from all those urban obsessions that our parents had abandoned up north. We measured time without the compulsion of clocks.

Our parents, refugees from Brooklyn, Manhattan, and Long Island, marveled at the absence of snow, the reliably cooperative weather, the simplicity of a life that required no shovels, no alternate-side-of-the-street parking, nothing by way of long lines and rattled nerves. It didn't seem real, this Miami, this asylum for retirees, fleeing Cubans, and deep-sea Southerners. What was the catch? How could a city that luxuriated in short pants all year round possibly be hiding anything?

We lived in this building called the Point. It rested on a small island half a mile from the ocean on Miami Beach. What was unique in those days about the building was that it was a safe haven for children and dogs. All the other buildings wanted to have nothing to do with citizens who were neither senior nor human. Highrises were the exclusive domain of retirees and snowbirds. NO CHILDREN OR PETS, the signs read as a sinister refrain in almost every lobby along the strip. This catchall tropical trespass—the brazen lumping together of offspring and animals—created mixed and mildly paranoid feelings of rejection among young families. These buildings were regarded as a last gasp of elegance in old age, a stopover before the "home." The Point was different. It was the Notre Dame of Miami Beach, a Jewish safe haven, an oasis for families unable to afford homes but unwilling to surrender their pets, or their children.

The Point was eccentric in other ways as well. Unlike those concrete-slabbed structures that rose up like towering mountains along Collins Avenue, the Point was off the ocean, surrounded by luminous bays and soundless canals. It was the hub of a residential area. A friendly giant offering shade to those Art Deco apartments and Florida homes that dotted the shoreline of nearby islands. A mammoth of white cement, a three-sided edifice with open vistas of sky and water, a great big P painted on a conspicuous crown.

It was also a madhouse of activity. The children ran wild, and so did the dogs, who forgot their station in life as household pets. Parents never hired baby-sitters. They simply deposited their children within the bosom of the Point, believing that the island would protect them. No one, least of whom the Point's management, ever bothered to enact any rules of conduct. The soul of the place would have risen up in rebellion. We lived unburdened by bylaws; the senior citizens living to our east knew what they could do with their signs.

All the kids realized that Matt, the lifeguard, was bopping some of the single women in the building, even the married ones. The sudden urgency with which he would dash off for his chemical box suggested something other than routine pool maintenance to us sexual sophisticates. LIFEGUARD OFF DUTY was one sign we did have, but it often meant something altogether else.

The very sight of that swimming pool became an occasion to jump in—for animals and humans, even with full clothes on. We used to play tag with the elevators, which entailed stopping at random floors, running out and tagging someone forcefully, then screaming, "you're it!" The trick was to get back into the elevator, leaving the scene and the stunned player without ways to rid himself of an unwanted pronoun. Then there was the tripping of the fire alarm, which resulted in a frenzy of mock fire drills. It wasn't a pretty sight, although it offered a few laughs. Older tenants would be forced downstairs, huddling in the lobby, wearing either pajamas or bathing suits—depending on the time of day. When everyone had convened, they learned what they had already known—it was all a false alarm.

Almost every kid pulled one of these stunts at one time or another. It was a rite of passage, a display of the necessary gumption to be part of the gang. Most of the parents didn't even mind. Occasionally one of us would get caught, dragged into the building manager's office, which was located in the lobby.

When it was my turn, the manager, Mr. Mendel, the young nephew of the building's owner, accused me of being the ringleader. Mendel was a sniveling bureaucrat, a small man with short hair in an era of runaway disheveledness. He didn't even have a tan. There was no doubt that when Mendel was our age, he was a tattletale of great promise.

"Mrs. Posner, I'm afraid that Adam is the one who is leading the other children in these acts of vandalism against the building. He doesn't follow rules very well, does he?"

"No. We like it that way," she said in that unavoidably painful-sounding German accent.

"But I could refuse to renew your lease."

"And I could break your head."

"Come, come now, Mrs. Posner . . ."

But before he had time to finish patronizing my mother, she had his head slammed down against the front of his desk and his arms in a full nelson, a fancy move she had picked up while watching Championship Wrestling from Florida.

Mendel never bothered our family again.

The Point also had its very own candy store, which drew all

the neighborhood children, as if the building wasn't sufficiently stocked with its own. It was a meeting spot. A place to become acquainted, and to plan the next terrorist act.

With all these children, the Point attracted many single parents. They had moved to the building in search of community, which often had nothing to do with their children, but rather a desire for ready access to sexual partners. Back in 1969, rebellion took on many faces of indiscretion.

I grew up amidst these communal diversions and the confusions of those illusory days.

"Come out, already," my mother, standing at the edge of the pool, would yell out at us. Her hands were holding tunafish sandwiches. It was feeding time for her son and his new friend. "You'll turn into fish," she said.

Our lungs bursting, we raced to the blinding sunlight that danced on the water's surface. The formation of our freckles grew in number. The friendship grew as well.

I was on my way to school this morning—all set to teach my class—fishing for subway tokens among a bunch of pennies when Brad called. Twenty years had passed since we had last spoken with one another. I had heard from a mutual friend that Brad was now living in a northern settlement in Israel with his Israeli wife and their two children. Wandering Jews, still wandering, never knowing when, or where, to stop. The Diaspora exists even on the soil of biblical beginnings.

"Hello, is this the home of Adam Poser?"

I hesitated, as I always do when confronted with that question.

"Do I have the right number?" he continued.

"I'm sorry . . . yes, I'm Adam Posner."

"Adam, it's Brad, Brad Isaacson."

There was a faint Israeli accent that he must have adopted in the desert.

"Brad?"

"It's me, man."

"You gotta be kidding. Brad from Miami Beach?" I said skeptically. "The Israeli farmer?"

"The very same one."

"Amazing. I've been thinking about you a lot lately." Not just a cynical, gratuitous remark. I had been thinking about him. During moments when I lose my geographical balance—wondering where I belong, and to whom—I reset my clock back to Miami time. I do it reluctantly, out of psychological necessity. A certain anchorage that inevitably brings Brad, and the Point, back into some temporary, uneasy focus. "Where are you calling from?"

"Kennedy Airport."

"How did you get my number?"

"By chance. I looked in the phone book and there you were. I was surprised to even find it. Kinda thought you'd be unlisted."

"In everything else I am. I like living an anonymous life. In fact, I've been meaning to take myself out of that book. Too crowded in there. I guess it's a good thing I hadn't done it yet. So what are you doing at the airport?"

"I'm here with my family. We have a flight to Rome, and then from there one that will take us back home. I know it's short notice, but we have six hours, and I thought maybe you'd like to come here and visit with us for a while."

"Brad, I don't know . . . it's been years," I said, stating the obvious. "There would be so much to say, so much catching up, and too little time. It would be too overwhelming a task. Better not to even start. We'll just wind up feeling defeated. Besides, I have a class to teach in an hour," I said, staring into a mirror that hung above the fireplace. "I don't know if I can cancel."

"What are you teaching?" he asked earnestly.

I didn't answer. My mind went on to other things. So many years since Miami. Another time, like a forgotten century. Unresolved tensions get triggered every so often, disturbing the fragile tranquility that I had carved out for myself. A long-forgotten birthday. An anniversary that suddenly slipped back into memory. A *yohrzeit* candle that went unlit. The sight of a seemingly happy family. All had surfaced more or less during the week before Brad's call. And this was why I actually had been thinking about him.

I buried my parents in the dry soil of a Florida cemetery, and I did the same with a marriage, which ended inside the dusty tombs of an old but towering Miami courthouse. Years of separation left me with no palpable feelings about the place. The memories that no doubt shaped me commingled inside the melting pot of my Manhattan existence. I could hear the breath of my childhood best friend waiting for a reply. I felt a tug-of-war raging inside me. I wanted so much to plug myself back into that world, and yet I feared where this might all lead. What was I to say?

Kennedy Airport, for god's sake! Such an altogether inappropriate setting for our reunion. Departures and arrivals occur with such frequency. My sense of balance would end up being only worse. There would be no time for meaningful reflection. Only a tease of tenderness. So unsatisfying. Such hallowed moments required greater respect. And however we might manage to make sense of our past, the solution would ultimately end up airborne— headed toward Rome, and then the Mediterranean.

But what was really keeping me from going? My class on contract law? Another day wasted in the manufacturing of yet another future lawyer? For this I should deprive myself of a much needed reconciliation with buried memories?

"Nothing that I can't reschedule," I answered finally.

I made a call to cancel the class, and then went downtown to catch a shuttle bus for Kennedy. Boarding without a suitcase, I appeared as an even more suspicious character than usual. My dirty blond hair had grown long, too long for the faculty's comfort, and now, the bus driver disapproved, as well.

Within the academy I am seen as a pillar of loose disobedience, a fixture of untidy irreverence. It is not at a law school where the snubbing of middle-class virtues and the defiance of middle age is ever appreciated, or even slightly applauded. Bowing to conformity—bending the spine downward in ways completely foreign to the anatomy—is the way of life. Those who teach rules slavishly abide by them. Most of my colleagues had taken up residence in the comforts of the middle class. They now lived in the suburbs. They were married with children. Volvo wagons stationed in their driveways, revved up for the next stop to Kentucky Fried Chicken, the Little League game.

But I had no dependencies—human or otherwise. I was alone in a one-bedroom apartment. A closet filled with motorcycle boots and an accessorizing jacket; silvery zippers and buckled strips adorning the shoulders and surrounding the heels. The cracked, worn-in leather laced the jacket like the inside of a catcher's mitt. Two-day facial stubble came standard on all my daily appearances. I was an unlikely colleague among the elbow patches, fashionless ties, and baggy corduroy pants of those balding academics. Among this parade of decorum, I was often mistaken for a narc.

"Give up the getup if you want tenure, Adam," Ian O'Malley, an important member of the faculty, once told me. "No one is impressed with that Hell's Angels costume. What are you—a law professor or some character off a movie set? Where's the Harley? Should I check your pockets for dope? It's time to move on with it already."

"Which would lead where?" I asked cynically.

"Where you want to be, of course."

"Where is that?"

My students themselves never know what to make of me, or I of them. A classroom filled with conquered Peter Pans. So young and yet already resigned to the vertigo of ruthless social climbers. They had surrendered, abandoned their most enticing personal dramas in order to satisfy their parents, or their peers. From the looks of me, it was I who was acting out some of their own escapist fantasies. The professor masquerading as Robert Plant.

"How cool. Just look at that guy."

"What kind of music do you listen to, Professor?"

"Party on, Prof."

Party on yourselves. Creatures of the spineless generation. Reagan's acquisitive zombies, joysticks fastened in both hands, and hearts. Linked by a lifeless umbilical cord that connected them in one bold consumer hookup to Wall Street, and then to those soulless suburban shopping malls. No wonder they stared out the windows so often.

For some I was the window, the man with the law degree and the rock-star persona, a taunting reminder of the racy outside. For others, I was to be viewed with mistrust and suspicion. The green monster, tempting their most craven impulses, laying out land mines that might sabotage their mission.

Who could blame their confusion? They were being taught why promises can be binding from a man whose life was totally unglued.

On the bus, sitting in the back, massaged by the roar of engines tuned perfectly to the bustling din of New York, I recalled those days in Miami with Brad.

"Adam, Adam," my mother said, tugging on the covers of my bed, my adolescent body, lying underneath, shrunken with sleep. "Mr. Isaacson is outside, with Brad. They are going to the beach. They want for you to come."

My eyes shot open, realizing what was soon about to take place—a race to the dawn, second time this month. There probably wasn't much time left. I looked out my window, eleven stories up, and noticed that it was still dark. Sneaking patches of blue were hiding off in the horizon, a sure sign of approach. The ritual continued. We were off.

Mr. Isaacson, Brad's father, was the first person who introduced me to the personality of stars. He watched them at night, picking them out from the clear, endless Miami sky. Often he would awake early on a weekend morning, scoop Brad out of bed and then retrieve me from down the hall.

Minutes later we were plopped down on the sand, without even a blanket. We waited patiently, our eyes straight ahead, staying alert for the slightest movement.

The beach was deserted, except for patches of sleeping lovers who had spent the night under the stars. Before the sun crept through the horizon, the sky turned a hazy gray, announcing the headliner's arrival.

Our heads tilted up, or simply looked straight out as far as the Atlantic would allow us. Sometimes we would just lay sideways on the sand, our faces pointed east, a lullaby of splashing waves rocking in the distance. Fighting off the lure of a warm, embracing sleep was a great challenge. But soon the sun would surface—piercing through our eyelids—reminding us of our pledge.

"Pretty terrific, don't you think, boys?" Mr. Isaacson would say.

"How come there aren't more people out here?"

"Yeah, Dad," Brad agreed. He didn't mind me sharing his father with him. Brad was generous in that way. He realized even back then what I was running away from.

"I don't know," Mr. Isaacson said. "People are too busy nowadays to appreciate the simple things. They have eyes, but they miss some of the best sights. Like this one."

Brad nodded.

The waves picked up momentum; their greeting became more robust as they hit the shore.

Brad's father was a hero to us all. Handsome and athletic. Sandy brown hair that defied partition. A deep tan. Confident smile exposing a gap here and there between chalky teeth. He was young—well, at least younger than my parents, who were old and beaten, and defeated by the Holocaust, and had no time, or interest, or faith in the glamour of dazzling sunrises. How unlikely for them to have joined us on the sand, bathing in the fragile light of the approaching dawn. Comical almost. Possessed of so little fascination with the celebrations of nature—its mysteries, rituals, curiosities. They had seen the worst that man, in *his* nature, was capable of producing. To them there was nothing noble, or beautiful, or sublime in the way the world worked. These were among my earliest lessons.

Sadly, when I was a child, it was Mr. Isaacson who I wished to be my father rather than the dark, brooding, tormented intellectual who headed our household. And my parents knew it too.

My own father was already an old man before I was born. A gray beard. An over-used, rounded back. The slowest of step. He had lived through many lives, seen too much, suffered more than his share. My appearance was not enough to shake his pain, or revive his energy. There was no playing of catch between us. I would have to find it elsewhere.

They were creatures of the night, of darkness, of another world. The Holocaust had forever distorted their vision, reprogrammed their faith, purged them of patience, created altogether new perspectives for ordinary survival.

I would run away from our apartment when the oppressive vapors of my parents' dreams invaded my own sleep. The pain of their suffering became too great—for them and me. Escape into the safe sanctuary down the hall. A place free of demonic consort. Devoid of Teutonic nightmare. The new technologies of gas and ovens were mere home appliances, not deadly weapons. Brad's parents were not ravished by nightmare and divided by darkness. They knew a sunrise when they saw one.

It must have pained my parents to realize that their only child longed for the normal life of a small boy. But they also acknowledged the limits to their parenting, shaped and defined within the dark side of man's crudest hour. Beyond the permissive imaginings of Dr. Spock.

The litany of precautions abounded:

"Adam, we will die someday. You must make yourself ready."

"Never show your weakness."

"Don't trust anyone."

"There is danger in everything. Find it before it finds you."

What they saw in the sun was an argument for zinc oxide. Nothing else. The ocean, fraught with endless drowning possibilities. Palm trees, falling coconuts. Unless the circumstances called for nuclear war or the avoidance of another Holocaust, they were unfit parents. Because these thoughts of Armageddon never occurred to Mr. Isaacson, they found him pitifully naive, but otherwise well-adjusted psychically for the modern, comatose era. If the seduction of Mr. Isaacson's home offered me a sense of place, then they were willing to indulge his early-morning enthusiasms. He could go on alerting me to the rituals of the sun, and they accepted my avid, respectful witness.

There were days when Brad and his father's rescue took other forms. The familiar knock on the door. When I opened, they would be standing there with baseball gloves dangling from bats that rested on their shoulders. Off to the large ball field at Golden Shore Park, just over the white cement bridge that connected our island to the rest of Miami Beach. Brad and I would run off into the cool green meadow of center field, away from the patchy infield, which was dried out and flaked with rusty divots. Mr. Isaacson would stand by the right-field line and hit streaming high fly balls in our direction. The scorching Miami sun swallowed the ball in its absorbing light. Our gloves served as visors as we searched for the ball's descent within the backdrop of a cloudless landscape. It seemed like it would never come down.

The ball might land right in front of us, like an unexpected trinket from the sky. Other times we backpedaled, legs dancing in all chaotic directions, our gloves raised high into the air hoping for some gravitational pull to offset the artlessness of our fielding. I remember once when, standing underneath one of Mr. Isaacson's launchings—a high pop that could have conceivably attracted the attention of NASA about a hundred miles north—the ball fell right into my glove, the weight of its impact causing my legs to buckle and give way to the ground. Overcome with bliss, I remained on the soft grass, the glove still attached to my hand.

"Nice catch, Adam!" Mr. Isaacson yelled from the foul line.

"Way to go, goofball," Brad said, offering his own support.

During the fall and winter, we played football on a patch of dirt that lined an elevated porch alongside the building. It was bordered by a brick wall on one side, and a concrete walkway that led to the swimming pool on the other. Along the perimeter of our playing field were sprinkler heads, sticking out of the ground like mushrooms. Our tackle football games demanded a ready knowledge of first aid. Being pushed out of bounds meant either a solid slam up against a brick wall, or the nimble dodging of a gardener's land mines.

We played as a team. Me and Brad against anyone. Taking on all comers. Tackle football, two-on-two. His slashing moves combined with my brute force. Many a time I got too well acquainted with the wall—a bloody lip, a scraped knee—but I didn't mind. Brad always managed to evade the sprinklers. We were unbeatable, and we looked fearsome. Especially with my zinc oxide, which if you closed your eyes and permitted your imagination some latitude in dimension and color, you might have thought I looked a bit like Dick Butkus—the black charcoal underneath the eyes, the unleashed aggression.

This family of Isaacsons. Unlike me, Brad was not an only child. They must have realized that to be an only child is to make peace with the inevitability of unshared loss. What possessed my parents to have a child at all? What possible experience could they have expected to pass on? All survivors must have contemplated this dilemma. Didn't they hold meetings? Propose resolutions? Wasn't someone interested in discussing the awesome responsibility of child rearing, and the disqualifying circumstances that would have made them particularly unfit for the task? Why burden a new generation with such an unwanted legacy? But once resolved to bring new life to this earth, why produce only a single witness to all that botched handiwork?

Brad had two older sisters. There was Ericka, who was frail and slender with dark hair and soft brown eyes. The family resemblance to Brad and the parents was unmistakable. Then there was Diane, the oldest. She didn't look at all like an Isaacson: squat with large breasts and eyes set apart widely, a flat nose that hovered above lavish lips.

The entire building was infatuated with her. To me, it seemed like an entourage of gawkers followed her every movement. The fact that she paraded around half naked probably only added to the intrigue.

I can recall my own early erections, and how they always seemed to point straight at Diane. All this a mystery at that age, and I, unfortunately, was left without sources that might provide a mature answer. I wouldn't have brought this matter up with my father—not with his frail heart. And I suspected that Mr. Isaacson, at least in this instance—with the object of my curiosity being his daughter—was the altogether wrong person to approach for sexual guidance.

It wasn't so much that she was pretty, but that she forced you to regard her so. Such is the talent of certain women who dangle alluring odors alongside their elliptical charms. It is not that beauty is only skin deep, it's that it rests below the skin, waiting to strike out against those caught hopelessly off-guard.

Diane was a creature of the Love Generation, and a poster girl for the summer of 1969, that season of sinfulness, mythologized beyond proportion in the lore of pop culture. An entire nation claims to have lost its collective virginity at Woodstock, but Diane's had already been long gone. Among her many outfits, Diane used to wear those low-cut bikinis, which she flaunted like a uniform of perversion.

Occasionally Diane would baby-sit for Brad and me when the Isaacsons were out for the night. My parents assumed that I was in good care with the Isaacsons—the people of the sunsets, the high fly balls, the more nurturing way of life. But they wouldn't have approved of Diane by herself. There was this boyfriend of hers, Joey, who rode a Kawasaki and smoked Camels. One day Joey wanted to go to a concert. Some of his friends—all on motorcycles—were waiting outside the Point, all revved up, a chorus of lionized machines. Diane was saddled with her brother and me. So they took us along. An outdoor concert outside of the Jackie Gleason Theater. We rode without helmets, holding on tight to the hippie motorist charged with our care. Racing along Pine Tree Drive, my arms were thrust high into the air, feeling the wind against my face and hearing my Harley chauffeur screaming, "Hold on to me, kid! You'll get yourself killed."

The concert was a fog of psychedelic smoke and pungent glue. Brad and I walked among rows of swaying zombies, the new order immersed in Dionysian revelry. Diane and Joey were off somewhere, balling in a clearing that had seemingly been zoned for such activities. We played hide-and-seek among those who were already hopelessly lost in trying to find themselves.

Years after the Isaacsons had moved from Miami Beach, my parents told me that Diane had been adopted. Perhaps that explained her romance with rebellion, that streak of disobedience that defined her every action. I liked her before then. When the truth was told, I liked her more.

I had often thought that I had been adopted, or wished that I had been. Left on that mythical doorstep, wrapped in swaddling clothes, a rueful note attached to the basket, mistakenly taken by the wrong parents at the hospital. Confusion at the maternity ward; the Holocaust survivors' baby wound up with parents of unconflicted pasts, and me, away I went to the land of remorse and apocalyptic preparation. I wanted, at times fervently, to link myself with the fictional parents who had abandoned me at the door of these misery-struck immigrants. I would have forgiven them had they come back—had they ever even existed.

Brad was waiting inside the terminal when I arrived. I recognized him right away. Despite all the time that had passed, he looked pretty much how I had imagined him, except for some of the improvised touches that nature had added on its own.

He was wearing an olive green shirt flecked with geometric arabesque designs. His two children—a boy toddler, a somewhat older girl—were huddled around him, occupying an entire length of a bright orange plastic bench, a retro-sixties sensibility, modernist chic. His wife—dark-skinned, dark hair, full lips with a moody expression—was seated on the floor, knees against the carpet, unzipping luggage and rearranging the location of garments and toys. I stood in front of electronic doors, watching from a distance, being ventilated from behind. Mine was a casual visit. I was going nowhere. Unhurried despite modern jet travel. The doors opened and closed. Determined passengers passed me in all directions. I looked on toward the Isaacsons with nostalgic heartache. I hadn't seen Brad since he was a boy. Now his infant son looked more like the friend I once knew.

Amazing how the generations make us remember who we once were. We yell at our children because we recognize some deficiency in ourselves, as though looking into a mirror and seeing the reflection of our own youth. The mistakes passed on, despite our best intentions, to our unsuspecting progeny.

Brad's face was handsome, those inflated cheeks that defined him as a cute little boy had smoothed out, the former freckles absorbed inside a rugged beard. There were some fresh lines on his face that seemed to point in no particular direction—neither showing maturity, nor the stuff of adolescence.

I don't know what he was expecting. A radical law professor? Probably not. What does a ten-year-old grow up to be? We are all imprisoned by the perceptions of those who knew us during earlier times.

"You look great," he said.

"So do you."

I visited with him and his family at a rest stop near the El Al terminal. There was a snack bar, and Brad bought some food for the kids. Small paper-thin nachos with drippy, *ersatz* cheese. French fries. Low-fat ice cream. His little girl was dark with large brown eyes and soft hair. She was wearing a blue dress with a white bow tied to the back. A child of the desert. She danced and skipped across polished floors. Her arms seesawed and whirled from side to side, some Asiatic or Mediterranean rhythm that looked so out of place amidst the raging hip-hop of New York. The little boy's cheeks and eyes reminded me so much of his father that I had a hard time acknowledging his presence. The meeting with Brad was difficult enough on its own without being drawn into a time machine.

Brad's wife was a regal-looking sabra, toughened by a life

surrounded by enemies. There was a no-nonsense way about her, an unveiled countenance, which Israelis have elevated—with some pride of purpose—into a national mask of negation.

"Brad says little about you as children," Ada, his wife, began.

"We were a little crazy in those days," I replied. "He is just trying to protect the guilty."

"Yes, but he lived an entire life before he met me and moved to Israel. I wanted to know more about my husband before I married him."

I looked at the children and said, "Too late for that, I'm afraid."

"It's not too late. I would like to know. He won't talk, but he says you could tell me. Why don't you?"

Brad glanced at me with sad eyes. Obviously there was territory inside him that he had not yet visited. What right did I have to open boxes that their marriage had already deemed closed?

"I don't think I can really talk about it," I replied flatly.

"Why not? What is it about you Americans? I thought you believed in sharing your feelings. Men with emotions are supposed to be sexy here. Men who cry make for good fathers. I read this in Israeli magazines. Such celebration of real feelings. In Israel this could never happen, but here in America, everything is possible. I watched television during our visit. People will tell their stories to anyone. The whole country! Oprah, Sally, Donahue—I saw these shows. The more painful and embarrassing, the more people they will tell. Crazy country. So what about you two? What makes you so different? What could be so bad? I've seen everything already."

"You won't be seeing us on Oprah or Phil," I said. "Nobody would care. Not sensational enough. Just life."

"How terrible a childhood did my husband have?"

"Adam, you don't have to say anything if you don't want to," Brad said.

"There they go, children hiding in the dark," Ada said, referring to the adults beside her. "Time to come out, whoever you are."

"I'm not sure I want to relive it, either," I said.

"Then let's forget about it," Brad said. "Talk about something else. Ourselves, the way we are now, today."

"It's all the same thing, really—here at Kennedy, yesterday in Miami Beach. Those days shaped us."

"Ruined us."

"Maybe so."

"You know I didn't call you up so we could go over all that pain."

"I asked you to call him," Ada jumped in.

"Maybe it would help both of us," I said. "What happened changed me too. It was an omen for my own loss."

"My mother told me about your parents. Really sorry. They were decent people. I wouldn't mind talking about them if you want, but leave me out of any discussion about my family. I don't want to stick around to hear any of that."

Ada grabbed his hand as though she were ordering him to stay. Passing along the hallway, a baggage carrier wheeled a large cart filled with mounds of luggage. The children were mesmerized, watching as though the man was following an elephant.

Where was I to begin? I wondered whether our childhood was too banal to reveal to a woman who lived through national wars fought on her own soil. What she didn't know was still shrouded in the forbidden. To tell the truth might result in us seeming like frauds, desperately clinging to a story that only seemed important because of the passage of time and our refusal to move forward.

"Well, it was like a time of lost innocence," I began. "The clocks just seemed to stop and our laughter went away. The whole thing was crazy. We were too young to figure it out."

I hesitated to go any further. Just thinking about the Isaacsons made me want to cry, and I hadn't done that for years. So, for emotional security, as a crutch, I reached out for Brad's daughter, who was sitting right next to me, chewing slowly on french fries. I laid my head against hers. She could feel my tears, which frightened her. As a curative offering, she passed me a french fry; tiny teeth marks remained in a sawed-off portion. There was a red stain of ketchup on her blue dress.

"We would sit on the staircase in the lobby of the building, right beside the bank of elevators," I continued. "The security guard would chase us away, but we would return. We were keeping watch. We would wait for Brad's mother to come back from her walk with his father. A couple of steps and he was exhausted. The same guy who used to swim laps in the pool and run us around the park now got winded so easily. The Adonis reduced to a skeleton."

Different but somehow more real than the walking bones my parents may have brushed up against in the camps.

"I should go," Brad said. He looked pained, as though his tolerance for this history had just ended.

"You should stay," his wife said sternly. "But if you want to keep running, then go ahead." She looked at me and said, "So what happened to his father?"

Brad nervously circled our gathering. The body language of inner conflict and confusion. I knew that Brad had been running all along. I just didn't realize how many miles he had logged in pursuit of open fields, in search of something far away from those Miami tropics, losing himself in whatever looked unfamiliar.

I recalled when my parents died. My sophomore year in college. First, cancer. A quick surrender to wayward cells that had commanded my mother's body. Before then I thought of her as invincible—the Holocaust survivor who had dodged death with an arrogant smile, who had willed the darkness to go away, to find a more acquiescent victim. Once Brad's dog, Corky, a German shepherd, made the mistake of barking at her. She barked back, then lunged at him, and scared him down the hall. Corky was to learn what Mr. Mendel already knew: this was no ordinary tenant. A survivor of the Warsaw Ghetto, and then Maidanek. A smuggler of bullets to the underground. What disease could possibly outlast her own battle-tested constitution? My father died of a heart attack a few months later, in 1979. The two of them had succumbed to such ordinary malfunctions in biology. And all the while I had been trained to await the unthinkable.

I was left alone, trying to sort out for myself the ambiguous transformation from college sophomore to adult orphan. In some ways I was prepared for their death. It was not through sunblock alone that my parents coated me for protection. The skin had already been hardened with tough talk. An adolescence of endless sermons. A childhood camp of psychological first aid. But in other, less obvious ways, the Isaacsons had prepared me as well.

"A month before he had had an operation for stomach cancer. In those days no one discussed death with children. And cancer, well . . . it was a word that we didn't even acknowledge—not even in a whisper. No one in 1969 had cancer, and certainly not in the year that the Mets won the World Series. But when our parents spoke of it—as rare as that was—it was as the 'big C,' which a child would have confused with Hi-C."

Ada looked confused. Brad chuckled.

"It was a fruit drink," he said, his first contribution to the story.

"When he first became sick . . ." I continued, with faltering pitch, "when he wouldn't wake us up on Sunday mornings anymore, racing off to the beach, chasing sunrises; when hitting fungo to little boys was beyond his physical powers, my parents decided to sit me down and explain death. They were trying to get me ready, for Mr. Isaacson's death, and yes, probably for their own. . . ."

It was a difficult lecture for them, and not because they dreaded the disclosure. They, of course, had already become inured to death, too familiar with its handiwork to show the least bit of surprise. And they didn't mind shattering the illusions of a small boy, either.

But Mr. Isaacson's end was not death as they knew it: so powerfully abstract, in which naked bodies holding infant children were shot and thrown into ravines, buried over in mass graves of anonymity. Brad's father was dying a real death, an ordinary one, far too premature and cruel and uncalled for, but still very much a human death. After all that they had seen, the routine death of this young, handsome, innocent, golden man with a young family frightened them as much as it frightened me. For the first time I think they started to buy into their own preachings.

"The world is not safe. Not for anyone," my mother would say. My father nodded his head in agreement. While these discoveries pained him, he saw them as a necessary function of my education. They had been teaching me to accept death on its own terms; not to try to comprehend its mysteries, or find fault with its logic, or challenge the irrationality of it all. Brad's father blindsided any of their former insights, and blurred their otherwise clear focus on the madness that they knew so well.

"But Mr. Isaacson is so young," I would insist, "he's not like the old people with their walkers and wheelchairs."

I was referring to some of the seniors who lived in our building. Occasionally an ambulance—its siren piercing the late afternoon languor—would roll up to the driveway and a stretcher would cart away somebody's grandparent. Sad but not tragic. This was different. This we had not seen yet: the death of youth itself. Unwrinkled. Vigorous. Mr. Isaacson was young and strong, always with a cocky grin, always with Brad hoisted on his shoulders. Brad seemed so tall up there, like a scout, looking out for what was ahead. Not even at that height could Brad foresee what was about to happen.

I continued telling the story to Ada and the mesmerized children of my former best friend. "As the days of that year went by, Mr. Isaacson grew even weaker."

The toll on their young family was extraordinary. It was as though Brad and his father were linked by some strange chemistry—the son deteriorated in sympathy with the father. Brad became lifeless. On the dirt-covered path that we had transformed into our childhood gridiron, we would toss the football back and forth. Brad's throws, which were always sure and spiraling, lost their trajectory. They would limp back, end over end like a tossed coin. Diane and Ericka were equally subdued by the coming of their father's death. I couldn't believe it, but Diane even stopped wearing those incredibly revealing bikini tops; instead she began to dress in a more ladylike and dignified manner, as though her indiscretions may have caused her father's illness. By adding a blouse and a pair of pants, perhaps she could now reverse the process.

A few weeks later Mr. Isaacson died, quietly, unceremoniously, at home. The family shattered like a broken mirror, the fragments of their faces splintered into shards.

"The morning of the funeral, my parents sent me over to visit with Brad. We went downstairs with the football. There was an hour before the memorial service. Brad and I went over to the dirt path and tossed the ball back and forth silently."

Pass after pass the ball floated into soft, tender hands. We never dropped the ball, afraid almost, not wanting to invite any further disruption into our now fractured lives.

The children drew closer to their mother. Sensitive antennae picked up on maternal distress signals, the awareness that parents weren't safe from scraped knees, either.

At the services, Brad was the wounded prince, the object of pity, the locus of the family's gravest misfortune. My father had taken him out to buy a suit, Brad's first—a dark brown one, a little big, one that he would have to grow into. The yarmulke that someone had handed him at the chapel presented the opposite problem. It was too small, and kept sailing off his head whenever he moved.

I stood next to him the entire time. I remember a group of mourners surrounding us, offering salty tears of sympathy. My father reached in and grabbed Brad, holding him to his chest, trying to shield him from the blow of the moment, the tenderness of strangers. The broken child was swept up so easily, drained of the capacity to even hug back.

Within a year, the family left us. Mrs. Isaacson was, as they say, casually dating, frequenting the places in Miami where the young and the lonely would go for companionship. She met a wealthy man from Englewood, New Jersey, a recent divorcé. Mrs.

Isaacson remarried and, with dazed children in hand, moved north. Fear of jobless, single parenting. A desire to abandon the once sunny scene.

But there was more. The abruptness of the family's flight shook the very foundations of the building. It was all bewildering, disorienting. A heavy cloud lingered above our once carefree island. The sun's temporary shadow made my zinc-oxide facial seem overly indulgent and wasteful. There was less chaos than ever, as though we had suddenly tired of it; time to check our watches, embrace order. Without passing a resolution, we adopted a meticulous and unfamiliar attention to rules. A certain decorum that had never before been practiced on the island suddenly gave way to the impossible—we had been converted into well-behaved children.

Perhaps it happened because we never got a chance to mourn. We never said good-bye to the father. We didn't say good-bye to the family, either. The haste with which they left our island produced a sense of their own demise. The way they once were died; our minds refused to unfreeze the image.

"A few days after Mr. Isaacson died," I continued, "Corky died. The dog just stopped breathing. I think that ended it for Brad. Faith was all gone. First his father, then his dog. Way too much for a ten-year-old. We then realized that my mother was right: we would never be safe, or feel safe."

When I looked up, my hands were busy twisting a paper napkin. Ada's formerly steely facade had lost its cool, as though she had left her post.

"Well, that's it," I announced. "I'm done. That's the full story as I remember it. I can't say I feel any better, though. How about you, Brad?"

Brad said nothing. He just moved his chair over toward mine, put his arm around my shoulder, and cried. He told me that he loved me.

Ada too was crying, the children clung to her legs like tiny life rafts. Something in all this had scared them, although they didn't know exactly what it was. Perhaps they sensed the vulnerability of their own parents—never a pleasant thought.

"I have seen all kinds of death," she said, "and still I find this so sad."

"My parents felt the same way," I said. "You think you become used to it all and the next thing you know, wham: the knees buckle, your body feels numb, your brain checks out. Death won't allow for any complacency. It likes the attention too much."

"So the family just disappeared," Ada said sorrowfully.

"Like a cloud of smoke—*puff*," I added. "None of us was ever the same after that."

"I never recovered," Brad chimed in, which surprised his wife. His silence was over. "After my father died, I stopped living. I wandered around so much. Nothing made sense. I was walking grief. My father was my best friend." Brad then looked up at me and said, "I hope you're not offended by that."

"Of course not. He was my best friend too. You and I were just hangers-on."

He started to shake his head slowly. "Everything since then has been part of some search. Like the funeral kept going. Life played out in slow motion. Even the voices seemed garbled. Nobody told me it was time to go home." Ada looked on pensively. She knew very well from what he was speaking. You can't truly love someone and not ache for the suffering to end. "I never really buried my father. I refused to let go. It all seemed so unreal. To live again would be to surrender to his death—which I wasn't about to do."

"Zombie land," I said. "I've been living there myself. I know how you feel."

"I've been smoking dope for years just to put me in the right frame of mind. I've been climbing mountains—not metaphorical ones, but actual rocks. For sport. All part of some quest. I think moving to Israel was part of the trip too."

"How's it going? Have you found peace?"

"Only with the Arabs—and not all of them."

When parents die, the children they leave behind begin to re-alize death as a suppressed horror in waiting. For years held at bay by the ramparts of youth. Suddenly the possibilities become in-troduced. Fear sets in. Unbending cynics kneel for hope. Mature atheists find religion. Death now scales the wall. Knocking on the door. The awakening of those next in line. The thin lining of pro-tection gives way to an all-too-cloudless vista. Brad and I clearly got a look at death too soon. And we were no better for the pre-view. One of us became a pillar of salt, the other turned to stone.

I smiled, and then asked, "How are your sisters?" I especially wondered about Diane. If Mr. Isaacson's death brought Brad this far without comfort, in what unimaginable ways could Diane find her own peace?

"Ericka struggled, but not as much as me. She was a little older, and became really close to my mom. Diane went off and joined the navy. Now she's a Jewish truck driver."

"You're kidding."

"No, not at all. She's one of the few women who do it. It's wild. A true frontier woman. She sends the kids postcards from all over this country. Small towns no one's ever heard of. Talks on the CB, cursing just like a sailor. I guess roaming the country day and night in an eighteen-wheeler is its own kind of search."

Ada interrupted apologetically, and said, "The plane is board-ing in ten minutes, boys. Do you hear the announcement from El Al?"

We didn't. "El Al flight six-seventeen to Rome will begin board-ing with first-class passengers. . . ."

"They are calling for us. I'll leave the two of you alone for a while and take the children to the gate. You bring all the luggage."

The thoughtful, but crafty, Israeli leaving us to shoulder the load. Ada walked over and embraced me. It was a firm hug, felt in the ribs. "Thank you for everything," she said. She then kissed me and walked away.

Ada and the children left. Brad and I shared what remaining

time there was. We talked about how we should stay more in contact—plotting our respective orbits back to earth.

Brad said, earnestly, "We should go right back to Miami . . .
start all over. Stand at attention at the beach, wait for the sun,
salute or something ceremonial like that."

"Tunafish sandwiches for lunch?"

"Yeah, that's right."

"I'm not sure any of that is back there for us," I said, checking
my watch, the countdown of our reunion now hostage to an airline schedule. "And besides, you're the one with a flight to Rome.
Isn't that where Jews first got lost? Maybe you have the right idea
about home after all."

"Well, actually I am building a house in Israel," Brad said, "all
by myself. Floor. Walls. Ceiling. Porch. One plank and nail at a
time. Putting down real roots for me, Ada, and the kids. I find the
whole thing to be soothing—therapeutic, almost. Maybe you
should do the same here in New York."

"Great idea, but the wrong city. We don't build homes here,
we're renters. The transitory life is what we call home."

"Maybe that's part of the problem right there," came Brad's
diagnosis. "You need a hammer in your hand. Come move to Israel."

"In Israel, wearing this jacket and with a hammer in my hand,
they'll mistake me for some Turkish terrorist with a guitar fetish.
I'll be in prison. That kind of home I already know."

We were afraid to leave, even to move. It was all a fantasy. I
began to realize how tied I was to this man. How much I would
have loved to run away with him. To link myself with him again,
salvaging what was left of my past and reaffirming whatever lay
ahead. We had taken separate paths, but were plagued by the same
sickness. For whatever reasons we had been reunited at this airport, at the El Al terminal, gate 4, we now found ourselves inexplicably closer. That at least was good. Because the tragedy of
Brad's father's death had brought me no closer to understanding
the death of my own parents. Like him, I too never recovered. Their

deaths only personalized the fears, and released my own psychic bouts with rock climbing and truck driving. Perhaps the isolation and the distance we had created from those times left us too unanchored from the essence of our childhood. We searched for the stars as children; we peered only downward as adults.

"I can't go," I said. "Even with you in Israel, I don't think I'll find myself there. You might be a key to some doors, but not all of them. If there is building to be done, it has to be here."

"I think we've made some headway though," he said, his voice rising, "for both of us. Don't you think?"

"Sure. We had a lot of catching up to do. And I think it was good for Ada to be a part of it."

"Speaking of catch, I bought a football in Baltimore. It's buried in the knapsack. You want to throw a little, like old times?"

"Here? At the airport? There are no sprinkler heads on the floor of the terminal. How can we possibly play?"

"Come on. Put some zinc oxide on your face. We'll find something to crash into."

He found a football amidst a canvas bag of toys and dirty diapers, then unleashed a wickedly thunderous first pass, which I caught, nestled inside the padding of the motorcycle jacket.

Back and forth the ball cut through conditioned air. We took short steps further apart. The last game of catch that we had had was on the morning of his father's funeral. Today, over twenty years later, the accuracy of our spirals had improved, as if gifted with renewed spirit.

"You should really come visit us in Israel," he said. "We can play in the desert. There's lots of room."

A JFK security guard approached.

"What's wrong with you, you can't throw a football in an airport!" he bellowed. "You two are all grown up, you're not kids. You should know better than that."

The man was wrong on all accounts. Besides, we were not accustomed to rules inside compounds.

"Sorry, sir, but it calms my nerves before I fly," Brad offered as an excuse. The guard pointed his finger, and said, "You better not be here when I get back."

As kids, when we were at our very best, we flouted the building's rules regularly. But we had now grown, and changed. It was time to go, anyway. We packed the ball hastily, knowing that Ada and the children would be worried. They were waiting at check-in, late for boarding.

As we waddled down the corridor, luggage dragging from behind, Brad said, "Let's take a look back and see if we left anything."

"I think it's a little late for that, don't you think?" I wondered.

We hurried to the gate, stopping before the metal detector. All the baggage crashed to the floor. "I hate good-byes," Brad said.

"I understand. I'm going to have to clean this new mess we've left behind."

"We have to leave, Brad!" Ada said with regained Israeli diffidence. Perhaps she was trying to make it easier on us.

We all hugged, and they, as one family, proceeded through the metal detector. Brad hoisted his tribe and his belongings upon his shoulders, and walked through the ever suspicious underpass. A tall man with a long nose and a drawn face surveyed the area. He was wearing a small earpiece. No doubt he was on the lookout for terrorists. He glanced at me for a moment, then his eyes shifted elsewhere.

I leaned against a glass partition and raised my arm, palm outstretched, offering a reluctant good-bye. The Isaacsons clustered themselves into the jetway. Just as they disappeared, the daughter ran out by herself, stood in the middle of the terminal ramp, and lifted a hand in a final farewell. She just stood there, as though fearing that to do less would be to lose me forever. Brad followed, smiled, shrugged, and then reclaimed his daughter. Using both arms he swung an imaginary bat, suddenly looking like the Mr. Isaacson I remembered. A fly ball of weightless constitution sailed high, headed my way, once again still lost in the glare of the Miami sun. With a one-handed salute I shielded my eyes; the other arm reached up, and snared the ball to my chest.

THE LITTLE
BLUE
SNOWMAN
OF
WASHINGTON
HEIGHTS

It was time for a story, Adam's favorite part of the day. The other children loved stories as well, but for them everything about kindergarten was equally beguiling. Blocks stacked into unsteady formations. Crayons smudged outside the cartoon borders of a coloring book. The discovery of a new skin, pasted over tiny fingers from dried glue. The obligatory warm milk and cookies, even the coerced nap.

But Adam showed little interest in anything other than story time. This was the one diversion he would allow himself. He could close his eyes, drift into that familiar trance of dreamy oblivion, and suddenly be somewhere else. Anywhere else. The most preposterous of mythical settings. Just not Washington Heights.

This day in Miss Dunkelheim's class was, as always, orchestrated with distraction in mind. Keep the children occupied. Feed them. Then send them home. Baby-sitting by mirrors. Adam already understood the internal logic of the curriculum—its maddening and numbing routine—so calculated to induce fatigue, to arrest the onset of rowdiness.

But his defenses were stronger, more practiced. Outside of school existed other lesson plans. Other methods of tutoring. Places where finger painting was not a priority.

"Look out for the bad men."

"What bad men?"

"One day they will come to get you."

"Who are they?"

"You won't know until they come."

"How will I know? Tell me who they are."

"That's for you to learn, but get them before they get you."

Adam didn't have time to play. He was busy with covert assignments—looking out for the other guy. Not the same for his comrades. They weren't about to resist the banality and breeziness of their inaugural years. But they were children. . . .

"All right, put everything away now, class," Miss Dunkelheim said. "I'm now going to read you a story."

Large bottles of milky-white glue remained opened, and an assortment of dull scissors, spread wide for cutting, now rested on soft green paper. One form of recess had been abandoned for another. By now all the children had rushed to Miss Dunkelheim's side and plopped down on the floor, right by her feet.

All except for Adam. This was his favorite time of the day, but he knew not to surrender so easily, or to trust any routine—even one that had already proven itself to be so prescribed, and predictable. One never knows when it is time to break camp, cover the tracks, and move on.

"I have a new story for you today," she continued. "I know you'll all love it."

What was not to love? Children's tales of breathless dragons and mischievous fairies. All those witches with spinal problems, and enough evil stepmothers to filibuster an entire PTA meeting. Heroes might live in chocolate houses with candy-cane street lamps mounted outside, just for show. Gingerbread always seemed to factor into these sagas—inexplicably, the building material of choice for residences soon to collapse. The roads could be yellow-bricked; other paths might be traveled by wolves. And there was no shortage of happy endings. This always made Adam suspicious.

He had his own stories, although he wasn't about to tell any of them. Why frighten his companions in kindergarten? So needless, and they so innocent. And who would want to hear these stories, anyway? Who would believe? After all, there was nothing made up or make-believe about what Adam would say—even if he dared say. His stories were real, the endings monstrous. And he was sworn to secrecy.

"This story is different from what we have been reading up until now, children, because this one takes place right here, in Washington Heights. If you look out the window, you can almost see where I'm talking about."

The children all rushed over to the window, climbing upon the tables and onto the ledge, pushing each other aside, angling for position. They tried to peer through the long slabs of thick and dirty glass. Black spiderweb-like veins zigzagged within the pane, as though frozen in ice.

"What are we looking at?" Kelly O'Donoghue asked.

"I don't see anything," Arthur Johnson moaned, "just buildings."

Miss Dunkelheim joined her class at the window, and pointed west, toward the Hudson River. She formed a plank with her hand and placed it between the glass and her forehead, squinting out into the horizon, over to the gray steel beams and cables that reached up to the clouds. "You see," she said, stretching over the barricade of commotion before her, "over there . . . the bridge."

Miss Dunkelheim was a slender woman, tall with smartly cut red hair. With her wire-rimmed glasses and thin lips, she had the look of a librarian. But she also had an easy smile and a face blanketed with freckles. At times she looked young and overwhelmed. The children never took advantage.

"What bridge?" Richie Morales asked, frantically searching in the opposite direction from everyone else. A runny nose was also adding to his misery.

"Over there, you see," Miss Dunkelheim said, readjusting Richie's head as though it were an antenna, "the George Washington Bridge."

Some of the children nodded.

"I see it!"

"So do I!"

"Now come back and sit down, and let me read you the story."

Miss Dunkelheim sat in a small chair, her knees tucked under her chin, her back sloped forward. She was holding a new book, *The Little Red Lighthouse and the Great Gray Bridge*. It was both a children's tale, she informed them, and also a true story—well, almost true.

Before the George Washington Bridge first stretched across the Hudson River in 1932—linking New York and New Jersey, from Washington Heights to Fort Lee—there was a little red lighthouse, which rested on the shore of the New York side of the river, at around 180th Street. Boats trying to navigate along the river—caught in an occasional dense fog or the punishing currents of the Hudson—could count on the sure flashes of light, and the booming tumult of a warning bell, to help them navigate through the channel.

The little red lighthouse was very popular among the tugboats, steamers, and canoes that floated past it each day.

Miss Dunkelheim read: " 'Hoot, hoot, hoot! How are you?' said the big steamer, with its deep, throaty whistle.

" 'SSSSSSSSalute!' lisped the slender canoe as it slid along the shore."

The children in Miss Dunkelheim's class loved to hear her read aloud, as she changed the inflection of her voice in concert with each character.

The little red lighthouse was the protector of those who sailed the river, a rescuer of ships in distress. Such heroism. So important a job. It was a lighthouse with pride. Miss Dunkelheim continued reading: " 'Why, I am the MASTER OF THE RIVER,' it thought.

" 'Flash! Flash! Flash! Look out! Danger! Danger! Danger! Watch my rocks! Keep away!' The bell began to ring. 'Warn-ing! Warn-ing! Flash!' said the light. 'Warn-ing' said the bell."

But the Master of the River would soon have a rival. Builders and barges came each day. The men set down massive steel girders and pilings. They attached swooping cables to towers that were as big as mountains. They were erecting a great gray bridge. The little red lighthouse was confused, and worried. Soon the work was completed.

The little red lighthouse stood at the base of the bridge, almost hidden from sight, dwarfed by the monster's grandeur, humbled by its own storied obsolescence. At night, a strong beam flashed from the top of the gray tower, searching the sky for the lost and the endangered.

" 'Now I am needed no longer,' thought the little red lighthouse."

But one night came a storm, with a thick angry fog and menacing winds that turned the river into a swirl of indirection. Ships ran ashore. Boats were unable to find their way. The great gray bridge called to the little red lighthouse, wondering why it was not sending out its light, why it had refused to sound its bell. The lighthouse believed that it was no longer needed, that the bridge's great flashes were more powerful than its own. But the bridge explained that its light was reserved for the airplanes of the sky, and not for the ships that cruised the river.

And with that, the little red lighthouse renewed its mission, patrolling the river, rescuing vessels that otherwise could not find their way.

Miss Dunkelheim read the end of the story:

"Beside the towering gray bridge the lighthouse still bravely stands. Though it knows now that it is little, it is still . . . Master of the River."

The kindergarten class at P.S. 115 remained silent as Miss Dunkelheim closed the book. She then lifted her head to see the faces of her spellbound troops. Normally one or two would have fallen asleep before the end of the story. The lilting cadences of Miss Dunkelheim's voice—rising and falling like the currents of the Hudson River itself—would have long provided an irresistible lullaby. Eyelids would grow heavy, struggling to stay open. Heads would bob forward, or backward; children would lean into each other and then doze off. The milk and cookies accompaniment, offered during the story, would only enhance the overall tranquilizing effect.

But not this time. The children were especially awed by this tale: the little red lighthouse, still nestled below the bridge; small, stocky but indomitable; a tenacious rescuer with restored confidence.

"Well, what did you think?" Miss Dunkelheim asked.

There were unanimous cheers of approval.

"Great!" Richie shouted.

"I want to go see the little red lighthouse," Kelly begged. "Can we, pleee-ase?"

Adam said nothing. This was not to be one of his favorite tales. The story was altogether too close to home—in both geography and plot. Where were the faraway lands, the jousting knights, the conniving wolves? This latest offering of Miss Dunkelheim's unfolded right outside the windows of P.S. 115. His imagination would not be sufficiently stretched. Adam wanted to be transported elsewhere—not to end up on Riverside Drive, so close to where each morning began.

A number of children found their blankets and drifted off to sleep. The school day was almost over. All part of Miss Dunkelheim's grand plan—the strategic segue from story time to nap, followed by the dismissal bell. Soon she would wake the children, and lead her groggy and stumbling brood down the stairs to the revved-up buses and awaiting mothers.

Outside the wind started to howl and pound against the windows. Snow was falling in great bunches of powdery slush. A crack of thunder ripped through the sky. Washington Heights stood ready to receive a winter snowstorm.

The entire neighborhood was overrun with hilly streets that toyed with unsuspecting pedestrians. Steep and unexpected drops were everywhere. A stranger, unfamiliar with the sloping terrain, might alternate between walking and tumbling about Washington Heights.

During a big snowstorm the streets became impassable. Buses and cars were left stranded; residents remained indoors—giving Washington Heights the ghostly sensation of a neighborhood abandoned of life.

And there was more. Menacing gargoyles haunted the facades

of dark gothic buildings. Laughing, crying, and taunting creatures occupied in various poses of impudence. Staring down on all those brooding German immigrants passing below. The children of Washington Heights knew not to look up, and they rarely walked alone.

"Miss Dunkelheim, can I stand in the corner?"

"Adam, what do you mean?"

He had startled her. The room was quiet and peaceful. She had turned off the lights while the children were asleep. She gazed out the window, tracing the fall of the snow. She was contemplating the little red lighthouse—the actual one, still there, under the bridge—when Adam stepped forward silently.

"Can I stand in the corner?" he repeated.

"But you haven't done anything wrong," she said in a whispered hush, not wanting to wake the others. "Why would you want to be punished?"

"I just want to stand up, in the corner."

Fragile child. His nerves had taken him prisoner, again. The parents had been in the camps in Poland. Selected for extermination, the death sentence pronounced by the master race. A new world order would be created, without Jews—only the purest of blood would survive.

Now their son seemed to know the horror, as though he had been with them—the entire experience coded in his brain, forever.

Miss Dunkelheim would always remember that day when she had taken the children on a school trip to the local police precinct. Adam didn't want to go. He asked if he could be left behind.

"I'll just stay here in the room, by myself."

Naturally Miss Dunkelheim wouldn't allow that.

"It'll be fun, Adam," Richie said.

"Yeah, they have guns," Kelly added, "and there's a jail."

"That's neat," said Arthur.

When they arrived, Adam, who had been dragged along despite a violent protest, mysteriously seemed to change himself into some other child. His eyes became glassy, his breath heavy, his small chest inflated. His fingers collapsed into irreversible fists. No one actually saw him make this apparent switch in identity. He didn't dart into a phone booth or down a magic potion, but the boy at the precinct was different from the incurably anxious child who attended P.S. 115.

The Central Park Zoo, or perhaps some other less sensitive outing, would not have inspired such a dramatic metamorphosis in a five-year-old. But this was a school trip to a police station. Instinctively Adam knew to be on guard. Police were not to be trusted. They weren't necessarily the good guys; they didn't protect everyone.

Adam also knew the transformative power of a uniform. The orgasm of influence. All those corrupting badges. The temptation that accompanies symbolic stripes. The precinct was filled with so much potential for abuse and injustice; he wanted, in some small way, to right the imbalance.

Almost immediately he became ungovernable. He didn't laugh at any of Officer Friendly's jokes. He kicked Sergeant Mulcahey in the shin, then tried to unstrap his gun. He slammed the gate to one of the jail cells shut, and even tried to free a drunken man who had been held overnight.

"Get that kid out of here or I'll lock him up myself!" the sergeant shouted at Miss Dunkelheim. "What kind of parents does he have? Didn't they teach him any respect for a badge? I ought to lock them up too."

Miss Dunkelheim sat outside the precinct door with Adam while the others continued with their tour.

"Maybe I should have left you back at the class like you asked. You must have known something, huh?"

Adam looked chagrined, staring down at the steps. He didn't mean to embarrass her. He just couldn't help himself. Adam had not been to the battle, but yet his soul feared the enemy—*some* enemy. At this stage in his life, there was not much difference between shirts that were brown or blue.

Miss Dunkelheim had met the parents. They were unlike the

other German Jews she had known from the neighborhood. Much more nervous, jagged, over the edge. She remembered talking to Adam's mother during parents' night. Mrs. Posner hadn't come to check up on her child's progress. She didn't ask what he had been learning, or whether he was well behaved. She had ignored all those notes sent to her attention; probably never even asked to see Adam's report card.

Her motives for coming were different, and inscrutable. She spoke quickly, as though in a rush to go somewhere, even though she had just arrived.

"We didn't want Adam to go to this school," she said in mangled English. "We looked for a military school. But there is none in Washington Heights."

"I don't think military school begins with kindergarten," Miss Dunkelheim said sarcastically.

"Yes, of course, but he should know."

"Know what?"

"What goes on in such places. Excuse me, I must now go."

And she was off, to the farthest corner of the room, pacing around edgily, waiting for the whole ordeal to be over. She spoke to no one else. She was guarded, alert, not wanting to give up too much information.

Others at the school were also concerned. Mrs. Turner had once been a real nurse at Columbia Presbyterian Hospital, but after retiring from that job, she now volunteered a few days a week as a school nurse at P.S. 115. She had silver hair and a weathered face. Her teeth clattered as she spoke, as though her dentures hadn't been fitted properly.

Aside from the routine scrapes and bruises that she treated at the school, Mrs. Turner also functioned as a kind of school psychologist. This was all before the days when parents aspired to raise the "well-adjusted" child. Child-raising was simple. Single parenting was rare; child abuse and molestation—of the acknowledged kind, at least—was even more uncommon. But there were always signs that something was wrong in the home, and Mrs. Turner prided herself on being able to detect them. Adam Posner's case didn't present much of a challenge at all.

"Strangest thing I've ever seen," she began telling Miss Dunkelheim in one of her familiar tirades about the Posners. "The parents have turned this poor little boy into a concentration camp survivor, and he wasn't even in the camps! You'd think they'd want to spare him all that." She shook her head in disbelief, then pursed her lips, which forced a few teeth to knock against one another. "He always comes in here, but nothing is ever wrong with him, except that his nerves are shot. I don't know what to do for him. All I have is a first-aid kit. It doesn't work very well for this," she conceded.

"I sent him down to you last week," Miss Dunkelheim lamented defeatedly.

"I remember the day. He was so nervous. I couldn't calm him at all."

Adam had appeared in Mrs. Turner's office, his blue eyes moving frantically, his short legs bending, his thin torso twisting, as though he needed to go to the bathroom. Sweat collected on his forehead; he looked sorely overheated.

"He begged me not to call his mother. He just wanted to sit with me and hold my hand. He said, 'Don't call Momma, I can't have problems.' But there was nothing I could do—he was traumatized. So I called her and told her to come pick him up."

"She came, didn't she?"

"Yes, but when she got here, he wouldn't let go of me, like he was afraid to go to his mother. And I didn't blame him. She gave him the most disapproving look. And she acted embarrassed. I don't like that lady at all. She said, in that condescending way, 'Adam, we cannot have such nonsense. You must be stronger. This cannot go on. What if something were to happen to us? What would you do? Hold on to the nurse's dress? She will not be there for you. She is nice, but she is a stranger.'

"Mrs. Posner looked at me, and said, 'Sorry, but I must tell him the truth.' Then she grabbed his hand. 'Now come with me, and no more with problems at school, right?' He pulled away from her and latched on to me. He was shaking. You think I should call a social worker?"

"I don't think we have a right to do that," Miss Dunkelheim replied. "They're not beating him, are they?"

"Yes, they are. There are all kinds of beatings that go on in this world. You don't have to leave a bruise to see it."

"Sure, Adam, you can go stand in the corner," Miss Dunkelheim said, the events of the last year having flashed back in her mind. "But are you all right? Did the story about the lighthouse upset you?"

"No."

"Is it the storm?" He didn't answer. She gave him a hug. "Everything will be okay. Your mother will pick you up after school and take you home."

Neither of them was so sure about that. Adam's mother wasn't always on time. Adam would often be the last of Miss Dunkelheim's children to be picked up at the end of the day. During those moments while he was waiting, Adam would grow restless, his insides busy preparing for all sorts of contingencies and calamities. Miss Dunkelheim wanted to speak to Mrs. Posner about this problem. The child needed to feel confident that someone would be there, that he had a home to return to after school. But the young teacher was intimidated by the enormity of the situation. Nothing that she had learned at Bank Street College could have prepared her for this. This wasn't a matter of not enough parental involvement, which was so often the case with troubled children. Perhaps here there was simply too much—of everything.

Yet, there was some strategy behind the Posners' commando parenting—bizarre as it seemed. Not showing up on time after school was one of their little tests, devised to gauge their son's instincts for survival. Could he make it home by himself? What if something were to happen to them? They had long ago warned him of the precariousness of life, and the possibilities—no, the certainties—of their imminent deaths.

"You will know what to do, no?" his father's favorite quiz echoed in his head. "Call Uncle Max. You have the number, in your head—always remember it. Tell him what happened to us. Then wait; he will find you. After you hang up the phone, talk to no one else until he comes."

Adam would often repeat this mantra, rehearsing it endlessly, committing it to memory, knowing that when that day would finally arrive he would need to be ready. He couldn't afford to forget any of the instructions, even if he became disoriented by grief and fear.

With Miss Dunkelheim's permission, he went to the corner of the room and waited for the school bell to ring. He was willing to do anything to distract himself from those yelping demons inside. Standing in the corner was like a reprieve. He watched the snow and listened to the wind rattle the windows. He focused on the alphabet, which was wrapped around the room; but now it seemed to be spinning in his head, a galaxy of letters—disordered and out of control.

And then finally came the bell.

Rrrr-ing! Rrrr-ing!

"All right, children, get your coats and let's form a line."

His coat was already on, a rich and bulky blue with a corduroy fringe collar. There was also a blue hat—a furry hunter's cap—strapped to his head.

They were led downstairs. Adam lagged behind, at the end of the line. The cold walls were covered with a season's worth of children's artwork: bright orange pumpkins left over from Halloween; the yellows and browns of Thanksgiving; white snowmen and red Santas. The sounds of little feet, outfitted in boots and galoshes, shuffled and skipped down the steps. The floors smelled of ammonia.

The children ran to greet their mothers. Most boarded the bus.

Mr. Walker was the regular driver. He was an elderly black man with a thick stomach and big lips, chewing on a cigar.

Mrs. Posner was not anywhere to be found. Miss Dunkelheim seemed concerned. She promised Adam that there was nothing to fear.

"What's with that lady?" she muttered.

Because the snow was so heavy, Mr. Walker waited a few moments before setting out. He wanted to make sure that all the children were seated properly. He was also waiting for the snow to let up a bit.

"Adam, come on the bus!" Kelly yelled out from the doorway, as though she were casting out a lifeline. "We can take you home."

Adam's lip stiffened. He turned his face away. He steeled himself. He didn't want the others to see his confusion. He, so obsessed with masking panic. But he wasn't about to get on the bus, even though he desperately wanted to. The bus wasn't part of the plan, not the scheduled escape route. Such an improvised, unrehearsed maneuver was unthinkable.

And while he didn't know where the bus was going, or where it would take him, a part of him didn't care. "Just get on, go!" a voice inside him said. Perhaps the bus would leave Washington Heights altogether. Adam would be forever in the company of Richie, Arthur, Kelly, and the others. Traveling over the George Washington Bridge, escaping to New Jersey, away from this undisguised pseudo-Germany, with its mocking gargoyles, trapdoor streets, and violent storms. And they could all wave good-bye to the little red lighthouse, purposefully anchored below. Maybe, in honor of their escape, the lighthouse would flash one final warning—a good luck sign—just for Adam.

But Adam had already left. He was crafty, a nimble hider in any game of hide-and-seek. Miss Dunkelheim never even noticed him leave her side. She was still waiting there when the bus pulled away—Adam, missing within its roar. Alertly, without incident, he headed home down Audubon Avenue by himself. Miss Dunkelheim finally turned around and saw that Adam was gone. All the children had been released into somebody's custody. Except for one. She raced back to the principal's office to report a lost child.

The streets were virtually empty. The snow began to fall even harder than before. Adam leaned into the wind, driving himself forward. Stores were closing. There was fear that this was no ordinary storm, but a blizzard. At West 170th Street, Mr. Wolf stood outside his shoe store, deciding whether to stay open or to go home. When Adam passed him, Mr. Wolf called out, "Adam, what are you doing by yourself? You must go home."

Adam was wearing a pair of Mr. Wolf's best snow boots, which his mother bought for him right before the school year began. Mr. Wolf told Mrs. Posner that the child didn't really need such a fancy boot. A lesser shoe would do, but she was insistent.

"He needs the best shoes because when the snow is strong, he should be able to survive outside."

At the time Mr. Wolf just shook his head in puzzlement, and then punched the higher number on his cash register. But now, watching Adam in the blizzard—the only human being in Washington Heights braving the streets—he better understood.

"Come inside, with me!"

Adam turned around, and with a two-fingered visor, saluted Mr. Wolf farewell. He then continued on his way. One block at a time.

"Call Uncle Max. Call Uncle Max—646-5958, 646-5958, 646-5958 . . ." he repeated, taking deep breaths before each choking gust of wind smacked against his face. A scarf became disentangled from his throat, and started flapping madly. He didn't dare look up, wondering what scandal the gargoyles might be up to on such an otherwise favorable day for torment.

Where was he to find refuge? Certainly not at home, but yet, that was his destination. The little red lighthouse would surely understand his plight: rescue his parents, or save himself. He had no choice. Much like the lighthouse, rescue was all that he knew.

At 167th Street he turned east, leaning back as he navigated with short tiny steps down the sharp drop toward Amsterdam Avenue. His parents' building was in the middle of the street, next to a vacant lot. The building was deep brown with an arched beige entrance. Fire escapes zigzagged from each window.

He ran inside the building, passing the large gilded mirror that stretched across the lobby, and climbed quickly up the stairs. Breathing heavily, he pulled on the railing to help himself up. The cold stone steps echoed as he attacked each flight. Adam passed no one along the way.

Once on the third floor he raced for Apartment Q, and knocked frantically. There was no answer. He reached for the knob. The door was open. Now inside he took off his hat, and called out "Momma, Poppa!"

The room was cold and damp, as though the storm had followed him inside, or perhaps this is where it all began. He entered slowly, afraid of what he would find. A trespasser in his own apartment. The living room was dark. "Momma, Poppa," he repeated, this time in a whisper. All he could hear was a swirling wind, coming from his parents' room. Moving through the corridor, he turned at their room. The door was already open. The room completely dark. By the window, two naked bodies were shuddering in the darkness. Two pairs of terrorized eyes—the withering remains of the master race.

ABOUT THE AUTHOR

Thane Rosenbaum was born in New York, in Washington Heights, in 1960, the only child of Holocaust survivors. His family later moved to Miami Beach, Florida, where he was raised.

After receiving his masters and then law degrees, Rosenbaum worked as a law clerk for a federal judge and then as an associate at the New York law firm of Debevoise & Plimpton. A number of years later he decided to leave the practice of law to devote himself full-time to writing and teaching.

Rosenbaum is currently a law professor at Fordham Law School where he teaches courses in human rights and writing. He also teaches courses in both Jewish Literature and the Holocaust at the New School for Social Research.

The author lives in New York City with his wife, Susan, and daughter, Basia Tess. *Elijah Visible* is his first book.